Meeting His Secret Daughter

MARIE FERRARELLA

HARLEQUIN
SPECIAL
EDITION

HARLEQUIN®
SPECIAL EDITION™

PLEASE RECYCLE

Recycling programs for this product may not exist in your area.

ISBN-13: 978-1-335-72457-1

Meeting His Secret Daughter

Copyright © 2023 by Marie Rydzynski-Ferrarella

Harlequin Enterprises ULC
22 Adelaide St. West, 41st Floor
Toronto, Ontario M5H 4E3, Canada
www.Harlequin.com

Printed in U.S.A.

USA TODAY bestselling and RITA® Award–winning author **Marie Ferrarella** has written over three hundred books for Harlequin, some under the name Marie Nicole. Her romances are beloved by fans worldwide. Visit her website, marieferrarella.com.

Visit the Author Profile page
at Harlequin.com for more titles.

To

Edy & Tiffany Melgar

A Truly Special Couple

With Lots of Love,

"Mama"

Prologue

Riley Robertson struggled to hold back the tears she felt welling up within her. She had known for a while now that this day was coming closer, but somehow she had still refused to allow herself to fully believe it was actually happening. That her best friend, Breena Alexander, was really dying. That she would not be alive much longer.

Stubborn, despite the toll her illness was having on her, Breena had steadfastly refused to go to the hospital. Either the new one built in Forever or the older one located some fifty miles away.

Despite Riley's endless pep talks—including this one—to try to make Breena see things in a positive light, her friend, sensing that she had next to no time left, had decided that what there was of it, she would spend it with her four-year-old daughter, Vikki. Even though, at this point, regardless of what she might want, her ill health was forcing her to spend most of her time in bed.

"They wouldn't let Vikki come visit me in the hospital, much less stay with me," Breena pointed out. "No, I'm going to be home for as long as humanly possible. Do you think you would still be able to look in on us from time to time?" Breena asked Riley hopefully.

Shaking her head, Riley, the first nurse practitioner the small town of Forever, Texas, had ever had, held her friend's hand. "Just try and stop me. I've got some time off coming to me. I can spend it with you and Vikki—" Riley began.

But Breena cut her off. "No, don't do that," she protested. "I don't want to take you away from your work. Just come by the house whenever you can."

Riley sighed. That was so like Breena, not wanting to put anyone out.

"You plan on arguing with me to the very end, don't you?"

A small, weak smile curved Breena's lips. "There's no fun in being agreeable. You taught me that." And then her friend paused. "Riley, I need to tell you something," she said.

Riley gently squeezed her friend's hand, not sure just what was coming. Breena looked so serious. Did her friend want her to adopt Vikki? She knew that she would in a heartbeat.

"Go ahead," Riley urged. "I'm listening."

Breena paused again, taking a shallow breath. Breathing hurt and talking was growing harder and harder for her these days. "It's about Vikki's father..." she began.

As friends, Breena and Riley had shared everything. Consequently, Riley was the only one who knew who Vikki's father was. He hadn't been a local, but a man who had come out on vacation from Arizona one summer five years ago. Matt Logan and Breena had hit it off instantly. They had spent every moment together until he'd had to leave to finish up his last year of college.

When Breena had found out she was pregnant, Riley had urged her to tell Matt, but Breena had totally refused to even entertain the idea. Moreover, she'd forbidden Riley from contacting Matt to tell him. She'd felt that since he was just starting out in his career, if he found out that she was having his child, he would give up his long-range plan and take a job to support her and the baby. Breena had absolutely refused to allow that to happen. To that end, she had sworn Riley to secrecy.

But now that she was dying, circumstances had changed.

"Go on," Riley encouraged quietly.

"He doesn't know..." Breena prefaced her words with another hesitant breath.

She couldn't believe that Breena had never attempted to tell Matt about his four-year-old daughter.

"Doesn't know you're dying?" Riley questioned uncertainly.

Breena shook her head and then said hoarsely, "No. He doesn't know he has a daughter. I never told him."

For one of the few times in her life, Riley found herself almost too stunned for words. When she finally found her tongue, she asked, "How could you not tell him? I know that in the beginning you had your reasons. But now…?"

Breena seemed to almost fade into her bedsheets right before Riley's very eyes. "The time never seemed right. This isn't something that you can just casually drop into a sentence," Breena insisted.

"But you didn't *tell* him?" Riley cried in total disbelief. It didn't seem possible—or right.

"It was a summer fling," Breena explained. "He went back to Arizona after summer was over and when I found out that I was pregnant, I couldn't find the words to tell him."

All sorts of words sprang into Riley's head, but she kept them to herself. All but one sentence. "How about, 'Guess what, honey? Know that perfect summer we spent? Well, it got a little more perfect.'"

Breena made no comment on Riley's summation. Instead, she had just one request.

"After I die, could you get in contact with him for me? Vikki deserves to be with her father. Or at least to get to know him. His name is Matt Logan."

"I know what his name is, Breena," she reminded

her friend, wondering if the illness was taking a toll on Breena's mind.

All sorts of objections regarding Breena's mind-set occurred to Riley, but she wasn't about to voice them, not now, not when Breena was dying. Instead, she asked, "Do you have a current address where I can reach him?"

Breena nodded. "Yes. But don't reach out to him until…well, you know," she emphasized, unable to bring herself to say the words.

She didn't need to.

Riley's heart ached and she felt tears all but choke her as she nodded. "I understand."

"Until" came faster than either woman had expected. Breena died only two and a half weeks later, leaving a hole in a great many hearts. A lot of people loved the kind, soft-spoken, young elementary school teacher who had died much too soon.

"I'm going to bring Matt Logan back to Forever, Breena," Riley said as she stood in her friend's bedroom, holding the woman's lifeless hand. It was already growing cold. Riley's mother, Rita, had come with her and had taken Vikki into another room to spare the little girl. "Even if I have to wrap him up in plastic and sling him over the back of a horse, I'll bring him back here so he can meet his daughter."

Riley swallowed a deep sigh as tears began to gather again in her eyes. For a moment, she was unable to speak.

"I'm really going to miss you, Breena," she finally whispered, her heart lodged in her throat as she brushed her friend's soft red hair back from Breena's face.

As she stroked Breena's hair, Riley finally allowed her tears to fall freely.

Chapter One

Riley could feel the tiny fingers closing tightly around her own. It only served to reinforce just how really small the four-year-old girl actually was. At the moment, dwarfed by the double doors she was standing in front of, Vikki scanned the surroundings, her eyes open wide. Breena had once remarked that her redheaded daughter's eyes resembled light blue saucers.

Tugging on Riley's hand, Vikki had motioned for her mother's friend to come down to her level. Riley obliged and bent her knee.

"Am I going to live here now?" Vikki whispered to her in awe.

Riley smiled at the little girl who had lived in the heart of town itself her entire life. This ranch and the house they were standing in front of had to seem like some sort of a kingdom to Vikki, Riley thought. It wasn't as if she hadn't been there on many other occasions before, but losing her mother seemed to have shaken everything up for the little girl.

"Yes, you are," Riley answered the girl with affection, "along with my mother and grandfather, as well as Rosa, their housekeeper."

"'Their housekeeper,'" Vikki repeated. Riley was just about to explain what a housekeeper was when Vikki concluded, eyes full of wonderment, "They must be very rich."

Riley thought back to the stories she and her sisters had heard growing up and she smiled. "No, not really. I was told that my grandfather and great-grandfather built this house with their own two hands many, many years ago." She smiled at the little girl. "Things cost a lot less back then."

On a hunch, Riley tried the doorknob. It should have been locked, but the handle gave. Riley walked in through the open door, holding Vikki's hand in hers.

For the first time ever, Vikki seemed rather shy. Riley found herself praying that this phase would pass quickly or at least once she grew comfortable with the new people in her life.

Closing the door behind them, Riley caught herself frowning. Despite all of her and her sisters' friendly lectures to the contrary, her grandfather had left the front door unlocked.

Again.

Their grandfather, Mike Robertson, just never learned, she thought. Or at least refused to.

The man had some serious explaining to do, Riley silently vowed.

"Wow," was Vikki's comment in response to what she had just been told. The little girl looked around as if she had just walked into some sort of magical fairyland. The ranch house was a two-story building and the ceilings were exceptionally high, making anyone who came in seem very small.

The little girl turned to Riley. "Your grandfather really built this?" she asked in wonder. "And he and your mom and that Rosa lady live here?" It was obvious that she was trying to absorb the information. "Mama and I shared one bedroom," she volunteered as if this was news to Riley. "Or we did," she added sadly.

And then, the next moment, Vikki seemed to realize that it wasn't news to her mother's friend. She sighed sadly. "You already know that, don't you?"

Riley never ceased to be fascinated by the fact that Vikki talked like a little old lady instead of a four-year-old child.

Breena had maintained that was because she had talked to her daughter from the moment the child had been born, addressing Vikki as if she had complete command of the language. It had never occurred to Breena that Vikki might not understand what was being said to her. Her friend had just assumed that her daughter understood everything, that sometimes it just took her a little longer than other times.

"Yes, I do," Riley replied. "And to answer your question, my grandfather and mother live here on a permanent basis and my two sisters stay here occasionally. Raegan is married," she went on to tell Vikki, "so when she stays over, she comes with her husband."

Ever curious, Vikki asked, "What's his name?"

"Alan White Eagle," Riley told the little girl.

"But your other sister isn't married, right?" It was an astute guess on Vikki's part.

Riley could only smile. The way she saw it, Vikki was beyond incredibly bright. "No, she isn't."

Vikki cocked her head as she looked up at Riley. "And you're not married, either, right?"

"No, honey, I am not," Riley confirmed.

It struck her as rather a serious conversation to have with a four-year-old, but she was desperately attempting to avoid the more hurtful topic—the one involving Breena's funeral. She had quietly buried her friend with only a few people in attendance. She was trying to spare the little girl so Vikki wouldn't be haunted by the memory of her mother's interment.

"And neither is Rosa," Riley added.

Vikki turned up her face toward Riley, curiosity in her eyes. "Rosa? Who's that?" It was obvious that Vikki had forgotten. It gave Riley hope that the little girl could be normal after all.

"Rosa is my grandfather's housekeeper and cook,"

she told the child, reminding Vikki of her previous explanation.

"The house needs keeping?" Vikki asked. Turning around in an inclusive circle, she was trying her best to assimilate what she was looking at as well as what she was being told.

Riley laughed, putting her arm around the four-year-old's small shoulders and drawing her closer to her. "Oh, that it does," she assured the little girl.

Mike Robertson, Riley's grandfather, chose that moment to walk in from the kitchen. A tall, muscular man with a very full head of gray hair, Robertson could still hold his own, putting in long hours working alongside his ranch hands. He immediately zeroed in on the small child standing in his living room.

"And who is this lovely young lady?" he asked, feigning ignorance as he took Vikki's hand in his.

Vikki giggled. "You know who I am, Pop," she said to Riley's grandfather.

It was a sweet sound, Riley couldn't help thinking. This was the first time that she had heard it in a while.

"Why, yes, I do," Mike declared. "You're Vikki, right?"

Vikki nodded her head. "Right!"

Going with the moment, Riley decided to make this a formal introduction even though Vikki had been here often enough—but, always before, it had been with her mother.

"Pop," she told her grandfather, "Vikki is going to be staying here with us for a while."

"And here I didn't get you anything," her grandfather quipped. He winked broadly at Vikki.

Vikki turned to Riley. She had clearly picked up on the word "us."

"I thought you said you didn't live here anymore," the little girl protested.

She was going to have to be careful how she worded things, Riley thought. There was no putting anything over on Vikki, even accidentally. She was the personification of the word "sharp."

"We never did anything with Riley's room," Mike told Vikki. "Or with her sisters' rooms, either. This way, we can spend holidays together. Or just have get-togethers for no reason at all," Riley's grandfather confided with another wink. "Would you like to join us for our next get-together?" he asked Vikki.

The little girl's expression had turned rather sorrowful, but she nodded her head. "Yes, please."

"Great, then consider it a date," Mike told her with a chuckle.

"I'm not supposed to date," Vikki confided. "Mama said I had to wait until I was bigger."

Mike exchanged looks with Riley. "Your mama was absolutely right," he told the four-year-old. "But as soon as you get 'bigger,' I'm going to be your first date."

The expression on Vikki's face didn't change, as if she was giving Riley's grandfather's words serious consideration. Then, after a beat, the little redhead smiled brightly and declared, "Okay."

Mike took the girl's hand in his and shook it as if they were sealing a formal pact. And then he repeated the word, "Okay."

Riley motioned her grandfather aside for a moment, telling Vikki, "I'm just going to borrow him for a minute, Vikki."

Accustomed to being obedient, the little girl solemnly nodded, "Okay."

Keeping her back toward the child, Riley turned to her grandfather and asked, "Pop, can I leave her with you for a little while? I need to pack up some of Vikki's things and I don't want to do it in front of her. This whole situation is all very new to her. I'm attempting to take this one step at a time," Riley confessed.

"Is that why you didn't have an official funeral for Breena?" Her grandfather wanted to know.

Riley pressed her lips together and clarified her reasoning to her grandfather. "I thought a quiet service after a little time had passed was for the best. I thought it might hurt Vikki less that way."

Mike considered his granddaughter's words as he glanced over in Vikki's direction.

"You never know," he quietly said. "She might have wound up surprising you."

"That would be nice, but I would rather not be surprised in a bad way. For now, I just want to let things ride," Riley explained.

He nodded, indicating that he could see that side of it, as well. In either case, his first loyalty was to his granddaughters and Rita, his daughter-in-law. It had been that way for the last twenty-six years. "Do what you think is best, Riley," he told her. "You know I'll back you all the way."

Ever so grateful that her mother had chosen to track her grandfather down all those years ago, Riley gave the man an impulsive hug. "I could always count on you, Pop." Her eyes smiled at the man. "I always have."

His glance washing over her, Mike pretended to look surprised. "You mean to tell me that you are just finding that out now?"

Her eyes crinkled as she smiled at him and patted his cheek. "Every once in a while, I have to review things like that."

With that, she walked back to Vikki, who was busy quietly orienting herself to her surroundings. She seemed to be studying everything carefully, as if she was seeing everything with fresh eyes.

What was going on in that little head of hers? Riley wondered.

She got down on one knee, bringing her face to Vikki's level.

"I'm going to be gone for a little while, sweetheart. I want you to stay here with Pop and keep him company," she told the little girl.

Vikki nodded solemnly. "Don't worry. I'll watch him," she declared. With that, she wove her small fingers through Mike's, as if she was going to watch over him.

A wide smile took over Mike's features. "I feel better already," the rugged man said. And then he looked at Riley. He had been the triplets' grandfather all these years and could read them like a book. Lowering his voice, he asked "the middle triplet," as he thought of her, "Are you going to be all right?"

"I'm fine, Pop," Riley assured him.

"Because I could always get Rosa to take over here and come with you," he told her.

"That's not necessary. I'm fine, Pop," Riley repeated a little more forcefully.

Mike inclined his head, indicating that she would get no argument from him. He retreated from the subject. "We raised you girls well, your mother and I," he proudly informed her. "By the way, after you finish packing up Vikki's things, what's going to be your next move?" He was curious.

Riley set her mouth hard, her eyes narrowing as she contemplated her answer. She looked at Vikki for a moment. If she had her way, Riley thought, she would just adopt the girl. It wouldn't be easy, but it could be done. And she already loved Vikki. She had since the day the little girl was born.

However, adopting Vikki wasn't the promise that she had made to her dying friend.

Her hand closed over the paper in her pocket. The paper that contained Matt Logan's address—if it was still current.

"Finding her father," Riley quietly said.

"Do you know where to start?" her grandfather challenged softly.

"Breena gave me his address," she answered.

Mike then asked the question that had been on his mind ever since he had discovered that Riley's best friend had given birth.

"It's been four years. Why didn't she get in contact with him in all that time?" he asked his granddaughter.

"My best guess would be pride. Breena was always a very independent person, even when we were kids. She didn't want anyone's help."

"But she was always the first one to volunteer to help someone if they needed help," Riley's grandfather pointed out.

That had bothered her, too, but she had reasoned it to her own satisfaction. "That was totally different. Breena liked helping. But she didn't like needing help."

"So, are you going to go to Arizona and drag this guy back by the roots of his hair?" Mike saw the surprised took on Riley's face. "What? I pay attention," he told her.

"What I'm going to do is write this guy a letter and tell him what happened. That he's a father and that Breena died. If he doesn't make the proper response, *then* I'm going to go to Arizona, or wherever he's living now, and drag him back by his hair."

Mike laughed, shaking his head. He could easily visualize that. "You girls do keep me young," he said.

Riley smiled. "That's just a side benefit." She turned toward Vikki. "I'll be back in a little while, honey," she promised the little girl, speaking up. Vikki solemnly nodded her head. "Until then, I want you to listen to Pop."

"I will," she promised.

Chapter Two

Matt Logan sat in his office, staring at the letter that had arrived for him this morning. The dark-haired man was having trouble pulling himself together. He almost felt as if he were sleepwalking, except that his green eyes weren't closed. They were wide open.

When the mail carrier had placed the envelope on his desk, he had almost thrown it away, thinking it was probably just some advertising material. Needing to compete with all forms of communication—texts, emails and the like—perforce run-of-the-mill junk mail had to become rather sophisticated.

But then he noticed that the letter was postmarked "Forever, Texas," the small Texas town where, five years ago, he had spent what was still, in his opinion, the very best summer of his life. When summer had ended and he had returned to Arizona to continue with his education and his life, he hadn't been able to get Breena Alexander and the three glorious months they had spent together out of his mind.

The more time he had spent with her, the more he'd felt that she was perfection itself. And, after giving things a little while to settle down, he had decided he really wanted to spend the rest of their lives together. She had managed to create that much of an impression on him.

But, Matt had come to realize, that impression had only gone one way. Breena, apparently, had had no desire to spend her life with him. All the letters he had written to her were never answered. Eventually the envelopes had started being returned, unopened.

Hurt, angry, he would have confronted her and asked why she was behaving that way. But he hadn't been able to afford the time. Matt had returned to complete his final year of grad school and romance, apparently a one-sided romance he'd acknowledged bitterly, had had to take a back seat for the time being.

So, he had nursed his wounded pride and forced himself to move on. Eventually, he'd only thought about the redheaded Breena with the laughing eyes once a day. And then once every other day. Until finally, he'd only thought of the beautiful woman and her light blue eyes once in a while.

His friends had done their best to set him up with

young women they'd felt were "worthy" of the man that Matt Logan was. But, in all honesty, he'd had no interest in these women his friends had found, no interest in starting up and perpetuating any sort of a relationship. The way he'd seen it, in his opinion, relationships were associated with pain and he had had more than his share.

So, instead, he'd focused on his education and then on the blossoming career he had chosen as an irrigation engineer. He was not the type to just mope and wallow in self-pity. That would have absorbed all of his attention. His parents, he remembered thinking at the time, had raised him better than that.

And, bless them, George and Amy Logan hadn't pushed. They'd allowed him to move on through life at his own pace. They were available if he wanted to talk—and were there in the background for him when he chose not to.

But right now, as he stared at the folded sheet of paper tucked into the envelope, contemplating what he would find once he read the letter, Matt was suddenly catapulted back five years in time.

Had Breena finally decided to reach out to him? Or was this just some miscellaneous communication of no consequence from some prince telling him that he had won five million dollars? That "all" he needed to do was to send back a check covering the expenses for the official registration.

But the postmark negated that thought.

Still, he fought the overwhelming impulse to crumple the missive and just toss it aside. Reading it might very well be asking for trouble.

After a minute of indecision, he carefully removed the crisp single sheet of paper that was inside the envelope and placed it on the desk in front of him.

Taking a breath, he proceeded to read it carefully. Not once, or twice, but a total of three times, convinced that his eyes were playing tricks on him.

By the third time, he was certain that this was no trick. This was definitely a letter of consequence. But not from Breena. This was a letter written by her friend, Riley Robertson. A friend that Breena had mentioned to him in glowing terms on several occasions that very special summer.

Selfishly, he had never met Riley because he hadn't wanted to share Breena with anyone. The time he'd spent in Forever, Texas, had been limited and he'd wanted to spend every second he'd had with Breena.

Just Breena.

Matt had felt that there was time enough for meeting her friends later, when he came back to Forever during the winter holidays.

Except that he never wound up coming back, not for the winter holidays. Not for anything else, either.

He should have, Matt thought now. He should have returned when he'd had the opportunity that winter. But he had honestly thought Breena hadn't wanted to see him. It was the only conclusion he could have come to when she'd never answered a single one of his letters. And he had sent more than a dozen of them to her those first six months. All to no avail.

After a while, his pride stung, Matt had decided that whatever he'd thought they'd had between them had only been one-sided. Breena had obviously moved on, finding someone else who could make her smile a great deal more than he had been able to.

But the words in this letter had hit him like a hard, painful punch to his gut. Matt continued to stare at the paper, speechless and stunned.

Not to mention numb.

The more he read the words, the more they hurt.

Rereading the words for what felt like the fourth or fifth time in a row, the pain refused to abate. If anything, it only seemed to bore into his soul and increase.

Why hadn't he just returned to Forever the first chance he'd had that first year? he upbraided himself.

He knew why.

His damn pride had immobilized him. His pride that had kept him in Arizona, safe from the sting of having his feelings hurt all over again.

And now Breena was gone and he would never be able to see her again, never get the chance to talk to her, to make her understand just how he felt about her.

But even so, there was something far more important at play here.

He had an offspring.

He, Matthew Anthony Logan, had fathered a child. In all honesty, he had no idea how he felt about that.

Numb was probably the best way to describe it, he supposed.

He had never truly thought about having children. Five years ago, that had never been in his immediate plan. Even now, maybe somewhere down the line, he could think about that possibility, but definitely not at the moment, not while he was still laying the groundwork for his career.

However, meeting Breena and, subsequently, the summer he had spent with her in Forever, Texas, was definitely throwing him a curve.

Until he had met Breena, he could honestly say he had never been in love before. And never thought about being with anyone on any sort of a permanent basis before.

That was why it had stung so badly to have bared his chest, albeit on paper, and offered her his heart only to have her essentially throw it back in his face. That was the only way he could interpret her not answering a single one of his calls or responding to any of his letters to her.

Matt looked down at the sheet of paper on his desk again, the words all but embossed on his brain as he stared at them, seeing them in his mind's eye more than actually reading them.

My name is Riley Robertson. I am a nurse practitioner at a medical clinic in Forever, Texas, and Breena Alexander was my best friend. I am sorry to have to be the one to break this news to you, but Breena died last week of a very aggressive form of breast cancer. We did everything we could for her, although she refused to stay in the hospital. She could be a very stubborn woman when she wanted to be and, as far as she was concerned, she had a very good reason for not staying in the hospital. Staying in the hospital would have separated her from her daughter, Vikki. Her four-year-old daughter.

Your four-year-old daughter, the letter emphasized.

He'd lost count of the number of times he'd read and reread that part. Each time, the words seemed to move before his eyes, refusing to actually sink in.

"I don't have a four-year-old daughter," Matt said aloud to the letter, as if that would just erase the whole matter and pull it out of existence.

But he knew it didn't.

However, if this Vikki really was his daughter, why hadn't Breena told him, certainly before now? Why had she kept this news to herself like some big, dark secret, or at least informed him even once about the child in the last four years?

It wasn't as if she hadn't had the opportunity, he thought grudgingly. He had done his very best to stay in contact with Breena that first year. But the woman had never responded to a single communication, not the emails or the phone calls.

Nothing.

It was as if she had ceased to exist.

Maybe, he thought hopefully, this whole thing was just some sort of contrived joke being played on him by one of his engineering associates.

But none of those associates even knew about Breena, he recalled. He had gone to Forever that last summer right before the end of grad school. And it was definitely before he had joined the engineering firm where he currently worked.

Matt frowned again, looking at the letter. He hadn't taken any time off since he had started working at Willoughby & Jones, and that had been over a solid three years ago.

He was due for some time off, Matt decided. And he suddenly knew just where he was going to go to take that time.

Matt debated whether or not to inform this "Riley" woman about his intentions. But, quite honestly, that was neither here nor there at the moment. The one important thing, once he ascertained that Breena was really gone, was to verify this totally unexpected piece of information that he had fathered a child.

A daughter.

He felt a chill inching its way up his back. He knew nothing about being a father, much less being a father to a daughter.

This had to be some sort of a joke. At least, he really hoped that it was. Because if it *was* true, it opened up the door to all sorts of problems. Problems he was not prepared to handle.

He had never seriously contemplated fathering children. Back then, thoughts about marriage had never even entered his head—at least, not until he had met Breena. But now, the idea of his having a child? That was totally beyond the scope of his thoughts. He knew his mother would love the idea of being a grandmother, but this wasn't just the granting of a simple wish and then moving on. This was suddenly a binding, lifelong commitment, one he wasn't ready to face.

He was getting himself worked up for no reason, Matt thought. Maybe Breena hadn't informed him that their heated romance that one summer had borne fruit, but he also knew she certainly wasn't the type to keep a secret of such magnitude to herself.

Yes, they had only spent that one summer together, but he wasn't some wide-eyed young hick. He had an keen intuition that would have alerted him to Breena's lying, if that had been the case. But that intuition had been dormant.

He just *knew* in his heart that what they had experienced had been real and true. While he couldn't explain why she had chosen not to answer any of his attempts to communicate with her, he felt there had to be some sort of reasonable explanation for it. Now that the struggle to get his degree and to establish himself at the engineering firm was mercifully attained and behind him, he could turn his attention to other things—such as solving this mystery he had wound up stumbling across.

This had to be some sort of misunderstanding, he thought. Or at best, he mused, coming back to this excuse, some kind of hoax engaged in by one of his friends.

Then he was back to the fact that he had never shared Breena's name with anyone. In the beginning, it was because he had treasured his little secret. And then, when things had not turned out the way he had wanted them to, he'd kept the incident and its details to himself. He had done it because it actually hurt too much to admit aloud that he'd apparently cared a great deal more about the young woman who had stolen his heart than she had cared about him.

For most of his life, girls and then young women had chased him. It had never been the other way around. Not that he avoided them. What he avoided was any sort of actual commitment.

It seemed rather ironic that the one time he had actually wanted to make any kind of a commitment, it had supposedly blown up on him—and now that hadn't been the case at all.

If he was to believe this Riley person who had written to him.

The question was did he believe her, or was there some other reason behind this "out of the blue" notification that had found its way to his desk?

The whole thing had left him wondering and more than a little bit confused.

He needed answers, Matt thought. The only way he was obviously going to get to the bottom of this, he knew, was if he took that trip to the little western town where, five years ago, he had first lost his heart.

And the sooner he did that, Matt decided, the better.

Chapter Three

Matt drove into Forever, Texas, slowly taking in the surrounding area. He wasn't really sure just what he expected to find.

It had been over five years since he had been here last. He saw that Forever had done some growing in that time, and yet there was a familiarity about the place he couldn't seem to shake.

Oh, there was a hotel here now, he noticed. That hadn't been there before. And, more importantly, Forever now had a brand-new, two-story hospital on its town premises. That meant that local residents no longer had to make that fifty-mile-plus trip every time they needed serious medical attention.

The local clinic, he observed as he passed, still boasted the names of three doctors who had been there back when he'd first visited the area. But now there were more names listed on the shingle next to the door. Several more, from the look of it, but he didn't bother pausing to read those names because that wasn't the reason he was here.

What really struck him was that the diner appeared to look exactly the way it had five years ago, although he noted that it had been spruced up. The diner, he recalled, where he and Breena would occasionally stop to have lunch.

Most of the time, though, Breena would insist on making him something. Raised on his mother's cooking, he was the first to say that his mother was good. But Breena had surpassed his mother, as well as anyone else he had ever met. Breena had been an excellent cook. He'd found her to be a world apart from anyone else.

Matt pulled his vehicle into the small parking lot adjacent to Miss Joan's Diner and turned off his engine. Pocketing his keys, he closed his eyes and, just for a moment, found himself propelled into the past. Five years to be exact. As he contemplated the summer he had experienced back then, an overwhelming desire slipped over him.

A desire to see if things had changed inside the diner or if time had somehow managed to preserve the small eatery.

He remembered Breena telling him that the woman who ran the diner—"Miss Joan" he remembered

Brenna had insisted calling her—had been part of the town since almost the beginning of time.

Matt recalled laughing at that. At the time, he had thought Breena was just putting him on. But she had told him she wasn't and insisted that he come in to meet the woman regarded as everyone's unofficial, somewhat grumpy, guardian angel.

Reluctantly, he had, and he'd found Miss Joan to be gruffness personified. Yet, in their own way, he and Miss Joan had gotten along. And, in his opinion, more important than that, Miss Joan had been exceedingly nice to Breena.

He'd quickly gathered that "being nice" was not Miss Joan's usual mode of behavior.

Opening his eyes again, Matt debated whether or not to go into the establishment. For all he knew, Miss Joan was no longer there, even though her name was posted on the side of the diner. That could have just been a tribute to the fact that she had been the one who had first opened the diner years ago.

In either case, he decided that he had nothing to lose by walking in. He found himself thinking that he could definitely use a cup of coffee to help energize him.

As he made his way up the front steps leading to the diner, it occurred to Matt that the steps could stand to have a little work done. Seeing them close up, they appeared to be a bit worn in places. He had put himself through college by doing carpentry and the lay carpenter within him now came to the fore, contemplating the kinds of repairs that needed to be made just to make the stairs appear like new—or at least not look quite as worn as they did.

Matt smiled to himself. His mother was right. He needed to learn how to relax, at least just a little.

That meant he had to learn how to kick back once in a while. As he reminisced, he realized that the summer he had spent in Forever with Breena had been the only occasion that he had done "nothing"—although spending that time with Breena had definitely not qualified as "nothing."

Beyond those three months, Matt was unable to remember a time when he hadn't immersed himself in work. However, very honestly, work was the only thing that actually gave him pleasure, not to mention a sense of purpose as well as accomplishment.

Standing in front of the diner's door, Matt hesitated for a moment, debating the wisdom of entering after all this time had passed.

Maybe he was asking for trouble.

More than likely, he told himself, he wouldn't find the woman here and, beyond Miss Joan, he really couldn't remember meeting anyone else in Forever. At least not anyone who stood out in his mind.

At the time, he had only had eyes for Breena and, until that letter had arrived for him the other day, he had felt that that particular mindset had led him nowhere.

Now, very honestly, he didn't have a clue as to what to think.

Matt stood there for what seemed like a long moment, debating his next move.

Should he just turn around and leave or—

The next second, Matt squared his shoulders. He had never run from anything before. This was not the time to start, he told himself.

Taking a breath, Matt wrapped his hand around the doorknob, twisted it and entered the diner.

The moment he pushed the door open and walked in, he caught himself thinking that he had just stepped through a time warp. A huge sense of déjà vu washed over him.

At first glance, he noted that nothing had changed.

The diner, he realized, looked exactly the way it had five years ago. He recalled that the interior of the establishment had always looked exceedingly neat and clean, no matter how many people were frequenting the establishment at the time.

Breena had told him that Miss Joan had insisted that the people who worked for her perpetually cleaned up after themselves and their customers. Otherwise, she gave them their walking papers.

For a second, standing there, he could have sworn that he almost felt Breena's presence beside him.

Damn, he swore to himself, he should have come back to Forever when he had first wanted to. He shouldn't have allowed his pride to get in the way and stop him when Breena hadn't answered his letters.

Maybe things would have turned out differently if he had followed his first instinct.

Matt resisted the desire to turn on his heel and walk out. He wasn't the type, he silently argued. He was here and he needed to investigate the diner as well as Forever.

And, he reminded himself, there was that small matter of his being told that there was a child with his blood running through her veins.

Was that true? Or was it just some elaborate trick being played by someone looking to make him pay for something?

He *really* needed to find out.

Matt's first inclination was to get a little table for himself. But that idea was quickly discarded. He decided that since he had made the trip to Forever, he might as well take a seat at the counter and see where that went.

More than likely, Miss Joan wouldn't even recognize him, he thought. Judging from what Breena had told him, all sorts of customers had come in and out of the older woman's life. He wasn't exactly memorable, he mused. There was no reason that she should remember him over anyone else.

With that thought foremost in his mind, Matt made his way over to the counter and took a seat.

Alerted that someone new had come in, Miss Joan looked up and then went back to what she was doing.

He was right. The woman didn't recognize him. But then, he reminded himself, there was no reason why she should.

Suddenly, he heard the woman's voice. She was addressing him.

"Well, look what the cat dragged in," Miss Joan said, her gravelly voice slicing through the air. And then she looked up, her deep hazel eyes pinning him in place as she observed, "A little late getting here, aren't you, honey?"

To say that he was stunned would have been an understatement. The rest of the diner and its inhabitants faded into the background.

"You know who I am?" he asked in stunned surprise.

The frown on Miss Joan's face grew larger. "Yes, I know who you are. You're the guy who came here on vacation, broke that poor little girl's heart, and then just disappeared as he went on with the rest of his life."

Matt could feel his back going up. "That wasn't the way it happened," he informed the older woman curtly.

Miss Joan liked the fact that Breena's former lover was standing up to her, even though she didn't like what had actually transpired in the end. Very few people challenged her. She would have been the first one to admit that she wasn't exactly the most easygoing person to deal with. She intended to make him work for it.

"That was the way it looked to me. You left her when she needed you. If I'm wrong," she said, lowering her voice, "convince me."

Matt saw no reason to explain himself to this woman. He hadn't even told his own family what had happened to him that summer. But he remembered the high regard that Breena had had for Miss Joan. She had told him that she'd looked upon the woman as a second mother. Her own had died when she was still a child.

Because of the way Miss Joan had treated Breena, Matt decided to let the woman into his world—to a degree. Breena would have wanted him to.

"You're wrong," he told Miss Joan simply.

"You're going to have to do better than that, son," Miss Joan told him pointedly. "Just *how* am I wrong? Explain it to me," she instructed. "I'll hear you out." Then, turning toward one of the young women working this particular shift, Miss Joan said, "Sally, I need you to take over for me for a few minutes."

It was not a request. It was a thinly veiled order.

Sally Rojas looked at her boss in surprise. Miss Joan *never* asked anyone to take over for her. The pretty food server looked dumbfounded. "Are you all right, Miss Joan?"

"Of course, I'm all right," Miss Joan informed her curtly. "But I won't be if you're going to argue with me. Now, are you going to take over for a few minutes or not?" The woman clearly wanted to know.

Sally raised her hands in a sign of total surrender. "I'll be happy to take over for you, Miss Joan," she quickly told the older woman.

Miss Joan nodded her head, her red hair threatening to fall into her eyes. "That's better," she told the food server before looking at Matt again. "Come with me," she ordered. It was obvious that she wasn't about to give him a choice in the matter.

Turning on her rubber-soled heels, the woman led the way to a corner of the diner located just short of the entrance to the kitchen. Gesturing for him to take a seat, she sat down opposite him.

"All right, I'm listening. Convince me."

It was an order and Matt knew he had just one shot at doing this.

"When summer was over, I had to get back to Arizona. I had my last year of grad school to complete."

"Did that require you going into solitary confinement?" the diner owner asked archly.

For a second, he stared at her, trying to comprehend what she was asking. And then it hit him that she was being sarcastic.

"No, of course it didn't. I called Breena numerous times. I also emailed her and sent letters. A lot of letters." Bitterness entered his voice as he went on to tell the woman, "She never picked up the phone when I called, never answered a single email or letter. After trying to reach her for almost a year, I decided that what I had taken to be the beginning of a wonderful relationship had all been in my head. Breena wasn't interested," he said flatly.

"So you gave up," Miss Joan concluded sharply, looking at him.

"No, I didn't give up," Matt informed the woman.

"I kept trying. But after a year of nothing, there was just so much knocking my head against a brick wall that I was willing to do."

"You could have come back to Forever over the holidays, or the next summer," she pointed out, a dour expression on her lined face.

"I had an extra project to complete and I was also busy applying to different engineering firms, trying to secure a position for myself. Besides, Breena had showed that she wasn't interested. I wasn't about to go crawling to her on my hands and knees, trying to make her come around," he told Miss Joan.

The woman took a deep breath, absorbing what he was telling her. She had had time to think about this situation and had developed a theory about it.

"Breena knew how much your career meant to you and she was not about to put you in a position where you had to give up something that was so important to you. So, in her opinion, she made the ultimate sacrifice by not telling you about her situation. She didn't want you feeling that you had to come to her rescue, sacrificing everything that you had worked for."

"We could have come up with a compromise," Matt insisted as the situation and its ramifications dawned on him.

"She didn't want to take that chance," Miss Joan told him. "So she didn't tell you that she was having your baby."

Matt clenched his fists on the table, bitter about

the life he had never had a chance to experience with Breena. "She should have."

"Don't you know anything?" Miss Joan asked, a hint of exasperation in her voice. "That girl loved you too much to have you sacrifice your dream for her."

The woman's words seemed to echo in Matt's head. He supposed that it did make sense. But Breena had deprived him of the chance of knowing his daughter sooner. What could he do at this point? He just had to step in and be a father, decide what was best for his little girl.

"Do you honestly think Breena loved me that much?"

Miss Joan shook her head, murmuring to herself. "Why is it that the smart ones can be so dumb?" she asked and then looked up at him sharply. "Yes, Matthew, I really do think so."

Matt's eyes all but bore holes through the older woman. Much as he wanted to believe what she was saying, ever practical, he needed more to convince him. "She told you that?"

Miss Joan impatiently waved away Matt's question. "She didn't have to. I have been reading people my whole life," she declared. "Breena loved you. More than you probably deserved would be my guess," she concluded.

"I'm beginning to realize that you might be right," he said morosely, honestly regretting not having reached out to Breena when he could have.

Chapter Four

"Don't you turn mushy on me now, son," Miss Joan ordered the young man sitting opposite her in a crisp, commanding voice. "The Breena Alexander who I knew fell in love with a man, not some boy with puppy dog eyes and a hangdog expression."

All he had heard was the woman's initial pronouncement that Breena had been in love with him.

"She told you that?" Matt wanted to know, eager to pin the woman down. The idea that Breena had actually loved him made him both happy and sad at the same time. But he needed to be certain that the diner owner wasn't just thoughtlessly tossing terms around. "That she was in love with me?"

Miss Joan sighed as she shook her head. "She wrote it in big block letters on the side of Riley's barn," the woman quipped. And then Miss Joan dropped her sarcastic tone. "No, she didn't come right out and say it, not in so many words," the woman admitted. "But there was no doubt about what that girl was feeling. And when she realized that she was carrying your baby—" it had taken very little for Miss Joan to put two and two together "—there was that legendary glow about her. No anger, no resentment, just an almost blinding glow. I can tell you firsthand that that girl was happy about what she was experiencing."

And then a wave of desperation washed over him. If he had only known, he would have been there for her.

"Didn't anyone ask her why she wasn't getting in contact with the baby's father?" Matt asked. He knew that if this had happened back where he was from, that would have been the first point to be made— urging Breena to connect with the baby's father, not soldier on alone through this.

Miss Joan shook her head. "Nope. Most of us mind our own business around here," she informed him. "And if they don't, they know that they will have had someone else to answer to." In her opinion, it was only important that *she* knew—and she had been quick to figure it out the moment Breena had begun to show.

Matt looked at the diner owner, trying to understand. Was Miss Joan talking about some higher power?

"Who?" he asked.

She looked at him as if he had suddenly become simple, although she knew that really wasn't the case. More than likely, he was afraid to allow himself to believe.

"Why, me, of course, hon. They'd have to answer to me. People, especially someone as sweet as Breena, should be allowed to live their life the way they see fit without anyone butting in—unless, of course, that person doing the butting in is me." For just a moment, dry humor curved the woman's even drier lips.

Now that the woman had seen fit to talk to him about the situation, Matt found himself with an overwhelming number of questions to ask.

"Did Breena tell you I was the baby's father?" It had never even occurred to him that the woman who had won his heart had been with anyone else at the time. But, logically, it was a question that needed asking.

Miss Joan merely smiled at the young man seated opposite her. Her smile said it all.

Matt recalled Breena once telling him, with a slight sense of admiration, that Miss Joan always seemed to know everything. That there was no point in attempting to put anything over on the woman because that would amount to an exercise in futility.

His next question, coming out of the blue, seemed to surprise the diner owner. Rather than ask any pertinent questions about the baby, the way she had expected him to, he asked her, "Is Breena buried here?"

Miss Joan's brow furrowed. "This was her home, son," the woman told him flatly. "Where else would she be laid to rest?"

"Could you take me there?" He wanted to know. "Or at least tell me where her grave is?"

Instead of answering him, Matt saw a hint of surprise enter the woman's eyes. He didn't think that his request was all that unusual, but the next moment, he realized the reason why Miss Joan's expression had changed.

"She can't right now," a very serious voice said, coming from behind him. "But if you really want to see it, I can take you."

Caught off guard because he had assumed that sitting off to the side the way they were, they were having a very private conversation, Matt swung around in his seat. He found himself looking up at an extremely attractive, dark-haired young woman with the most intense blue eyes he had ever seen.

There wasn't a hint of a smile on the woman's face. As a matter of fact, outside of Miss Joan, Matt couldn't recall ever seeing anyone looking so intensely dour before.

He stared at her. No introductions had been made, so he took it upon himself to ask. "I'm sorry, you are...?"

Riley shifted, making her way around his side of the table to face the man Miss Joan was talking to. She didn't need any introductions made.

She knew.

"Incredibly surprised that you actually turned up," she finally replied.

Finding himself at a complete disadvantage, Matt looked to Miss Joan for enlightenment. Right now, like the old line said, Matt felt as if he was suddenly caught between the devil and the deep blue sea. Neither option would have been of his own choosing, but since he had come to Forever, he would be the first to admit that he needed things cleared up. The faster that happened, the faster he would be able to get away from the unnerving glare of these disapproving women.

Not only that, the faster he could get to the reason he had come here in the first place.

He wanted to visit Breena's grave and say goodbye to her. Until he did that, part of this just wouldn't seem real to him.

For Matt's benefit, Miss Joan nodded toward the young woman who had joined them and made the necessary introductions.

"This is Riley Robertson, Forever's first nurse practitioner as well as Breena's best friend. She's the one who wrote to you," Miss Joan added simply.

"I should have picked that up from her tone." Matt addressed the words to Miss Joan, not to the woman who was glaring at him.

Miss Joan made no comment. "And this, of course, is Matt Logan. Okay, you two," she went on, her hazel eyes sweeping over them, "shake hands and go back to your corners." Miss Joan paused and said in a more forceful voice, "Breena would have expected that from the two of you."

And then the diner owner picked up on Riley's offer. "Why don't you take Matt over to see Breena's grave?" She stressed pointedly, "After all, he did ask to see it."

There was no room for argument in the tone she used.

Riley now looked reluctant to make good on her initial offer. Still, the nurse practitioner supposed she should go along with Miss Joan's so-called "suggestion."

"If he really wants to see the grave," Riley qualified, "I can take him."

"He really wants to see it," Miss Joan declared in her no-nonsense voice. And then she gave Matt a look that dared him to disagree with her. "Right?"

"Right," he replied, but not because he was intimidated. It was because it was the truth.

From the moment he had heard that Breena had died, Matt had felt bereft, like someone had dug a hole in his heart using an extremely jagged spoon. The realization that she was permanently gone from this earth, that he would never see her smiling face again, no matter what he did, had hit him with the force of a small nuclear bomb going off.

Again he upbraided himself for not returning to Forever that first winter, or at least the following summer; for allowing his pride to make him inert. He had actually talked himself into believing that he was being kind to Breena by refraining from making any sort of contact. That was what she'd wanted, he'd thought, so that was what she was going to get—a complete break from him.

Idiot, he silently chastised himself. What the hell had he been thinking to believe that?

Riley turned toward Matt. "You ready?" she asked as she prepared to drive the stranger who had broken her best friend's heart so he could "visit" her in the graveyard.

"Ready," Matt answered, his voice monotonic, almost flat.

She led the way out.

The trip from Miss Joan's Diner to the graveyard was a short one, but even so, Riley found that she had to bite her tongue a number of times to keep from saying the words that kept rising to her lips.

She desperately wanted to take this man to task, to demand to know why he hadn't gotten in touch with Breena in the last four years. Maybe Breena hadn't answered any of his letters, or emails, or his phone calls, but that still wasn't an excuse to give up or to ignore her. The man knew where she lived, he could have easily flown out or even driven to come see her.

Why hadn't he?

When Breena had talked about him—and she'd talked about the man in the warmest of terms—it was obvious that she'd cared about him and that they had parted on the best of terms.

Why had she been so stubborn? The excuse she used just didn't make sense.

There had been several times that Riley had had to talk herself out of taking the bull by the horns and contacting the man herself. That first year, she had figured out where he lived by taking notice of the postmark on one of his letters. But she'd known that Breena would have taken it as a sign of betrayal if she had butted in. So, as much as she had wanted to reach out to Matt Logan, she hadn't.

But, looking back now, she had never regretted anything so much in her life, Riley thought. If nothing else, Breena would have been happy those last years of her life.

Signaling to the right, Riley pulled up into the immaculately tended graveyard. She parked her vehicle just outside the main, marble-framed entrance.

"Breena's grave is located over there on the far end," she informed Matt as she got out of the car.

Riley waited for the man who had captured Breena's heart to join her, then led the way through the myriad headstones and statues until she came to a stop in front of a lovely, newly installed statue of an angel with a touching, innocent expression. The angel was looking up toward the sky.

Matt took note of the general surrounding area. "This is nice," Matt said quietly, almost to himself.

Riley thought he was referring to the statue. "We all chipped in," she heard herself telling him before she could stop.

"'We'?" Matt asked, waiting for Riley to elaborate.

"My family and I, and Miss Joan." She could see that he was waiting for more elaboration. "We didn't want too many people to know about what we were doing until it was done," Riley explained. "Breena didn't like too much attention being focused on her."

Looking at the headstone in front of the statue, Matt nodded. "Yes, I remember that about her," he said solemnly. "Everything was always about everyone else. It was never about her."

Again he couldn't help thinking that he should have been there for her. Breena shouldn't have had to have gone through this alone.

But then, he realized in the next moment, Breena hadn't had to face this on her own. He was beginning to see that Breena had had a great many people around her who had cared about her, people who were more than willing to be there for her.

She was, Matt caught himself thinking, a very, very special person.

He could feel Riley staring at him even as he was looking at the statue that had been erected. A statue that he realized looked a good deal like Breena.

Questions crowded in his head, almost making it throb.

He suddenly felt closer to Breena than he had in the last five years.

"Was she in pain?" he heard himself ask quietly.

The question took her by surprise. For the last few years, she had thought of Matt as being too into himself to be capable of anything as sensitive as the question he had just asked.

Thinking that maybe she had misheard him, Riley asked, "What was that?"

"Was she in pain?" he asked more loudly. "Toward the end, was Breena in pain? Did she suffer?" He wanted to know, even though voicing the question hurt.

She could only tell him what she knew. "Breena never complained," Riley told him. "But then, complaining wasn't her way. There were a few times, near the end, when I could see the pain in her face, but whenever I asked her about it, she just denied it. That was Breena," she said with a touch of pride. "A brave soldier to the very end."

Matt looked down at the grave and Riley realized in surprise that he was obviously fighting back tears. Her opinion of him began to soften.

"I really wish I had known," he murmured softly with a wave of regret.

Now that he had said it, that he sounded as if he was regretting the way things had played themselves out, Riley had managed to dispense the anger that had been pounding so hard in her chest just a few moments ago.

Riley understood that she couldn't hold the situation against him, especially not if he was holding it against himself, and now that she took note of it, the man did look upset about the way things had played themselves out.

Riley blew out a breath. She had to admit that her heart went out to him.

"She didn't want you to know, not until she was gone," she reminded Matt.

But he shook his head, dismissing the explanation. He couldn't accept that excuse.

"Someone should have said something to me."

Chapter Five

"I thought about it," Riley admitted.

"Then why didn't you reach out to me?" He was curious. "You were probably close enough to Breena to be able to find my address."

"Because my loyalty was to Breena, not you, and she didn't want me to 'summon' you," she told him simply. "I have to admit that hindsight has me regretting that I didn't get in contact with you," she said. "But we can't go back and change things, we can only move forward."

Riley pressed her lips together, taking note of the sorrow that she saw in Matt's eyes as he looked at Breena's gravesite. "Would you like some time alone?" she asked, nodding toward Breena's headstone. She pointed to the left. "I can go over there and wait for you."

The offer struck him as being very kind and understanding. He had to admit that coming from the woman who had been scowling at him, it did take him by surprise. Matt cleared his throat, realizing that his emotions had welled up within him and momentarily making it difficult for him to talk. It took him a second to be able to pull himself together. "That would be very nice of you," he said rather stiffly. "I would appreciate that."

Without a word, Riley retreated to the side, giving the man who had swept Breena off her feet his space alone with her memory.

Matt stood there in silence for a moment, looking down at Breena's grave. A flood of words and emotions all crowded in his head, vying for space.

"Why didn't you let me know what you were going through?" he whispered to the woman who had been laid to rest here. The woman who, for the short space of a few months, he had fancied himself spending the rest of his life with. "I loved you, you know," he continued, the weight of his words pressing against his chest, making it difficult for him to breathe. "Really loved you. And it was no secret that I had never felt that way before," he confided in a tortured whisper.

Another wave of emotions wrestled for space within him. He struggled to keep the tears that were in his eyes from falling.

Damn it, Matt thought angrily. This wasn't fair. He shouldn't be standing here, talking to a head-stone. He should be planning the rest of his life with Breena, not contemplating—now that Riley had told him that Breena had confided that she'd loved him—how he was going to face the rest of his life without her.

He knew the way of the world, knew that people suffered losses and moved on. But he had never thought that he would be one of those people.

Matt had honestly believed that if he were one of those people who was lucky enough to stumble across love, then the rest would just work itself out, not fade away into oblivion.

This wasn't fair, he caught himself thinking again, clenching his fists at his sides.

It wasn't fair at all.

Riley fully intended to give Matt his space for as long as he needed it and just occupy her thoughts with something else. But she wasn't able to simply tear her thoughts away and focus on that something else. The sight of Matt's shoulders looking so down-cast had really gotten to her.

She had spent the last four years calling the man names in her head every chance she had. She'd found herself being furious at the way he had ultimately treated her best friend, apparently just forgetting about her. But now Riley realized that she had been wrong. Very wrong. Matt hadn't just moved on with his life and turned his back on Breena. No matter how she played this out in her mind, Matt was not the one to blame for this miscommunication.

Breena was.

She had done him a disservice, she thought, guilt burrowing through her.

The next moment, she saw Matt looking in her direction as he walked away from the gravesite. Her heart went out to him.

An idea occurred to her. "Are you ready to go?" she asked Matt.

He shrugged vaguely. Although his heart ached, he couldn't just stand there having a conversation with someone who wasn't really there.

"Yeah, sure," he answered.

"Can I interest you in a late lunch or an early dinner?" she asked him as Matt followed her to her vehicle.

"You mean at the diner?" he queried, thinking she was going to take him back to Miss Joan's. Right now, feeling too raw to deal with the sharp-tongued woman, the idea didn't appeal to him.

"No, not the diner," she told him. "I was thinking of taking you to my grandfather's ranch," Riley said and then explained. "He expressed a desire to meet you."

Matt looked at her, confusion furrowing his brow. "Why would he want to meet me?"

"Because," she said, getting in behind the steering wheel of her car, "like everyone else, my grandfather cared a great deal about Breena." She put it in the best terms that she could. "Pop just wants to meet the man who had captured her heart."

"No, I didn't capture her heart," Matt protested, "because if that had been true, I would have gotten her to marry me."

About to start her car, Riley's hand froze in midair as she stared at the man in the passenger seat. "Did you actually outright ask her to marry you?" This was something that Breena had never just come out and told her. Her friend had kept the nature of their communication before he'd left to go back to grad school that year to herself.

"Well, no I didn't, but I would have if she had only answered any of my letters or calls or emails. But she didn't," he said with a heartbreaking finality.

"That was because she knew right off the bat that she was pregnant and she didn't want you to feel obligated to marry her."

He looked at her skeptically. "How could she have known she was pregnant so quickly?"

"All that matters was that she did," Riley told him. "And she was right. As far as you go, all you need to focus on was that, when it came to you, Breena had the best of intentions."

He sighed, far from happy with Riley's assessment. "Well, we all know how that turned out," Matt concluded dourly.

She didn't want to go on sparring with him over this. "You didn't answer my question about whether you are up for a late lunch or want an early dinner instead," she reminded him.

What he wanted was to be alone with his thoughts. "Neither," Matt told the woman.

"Sorry, but the time for refusals has passed," she said flippantly. "Right now, you need to choose one or the other."

He eyed her as if he thought she was putting him on. However one glance at her face told him that she was being serious.

"And your father's actually all right with this, with you springing a stranger on him?" he asked skeptically.

He wasn't listening to her, Riley thought, annoyed. "I told you, my grandfather cared about Breena—the same way that we all did. And because of that, he wants to meet you," she informed him.

When he didn't answer after a beat, Riley made the decision for the man. "You're having dinner at our place."

Matt's brow creased. "I thought you said you didn't live there," he returned, recalling their previous conversation on the subject.

"I should have clarified that we all grew up in my grandfather's house and, even after we moved out, we still all think of his house as ours, as well," she explained.

"'We'?" Matt repeated, caught by her phraseology. "Just how many people are there in a 'we'?"

She directed a completely unreadable smile his way. "You'll find out."

There was a reason for her evasive answer. If Breena hadn't shared with him that her best friend was one of triplets, she wasn't about to spring that on him at this point. It wasn't exactly the easiest thing to come to terms with. Besides, Riley reasoned, she didn't want to have him distracted at a time like this. She knew that meeting his daughter for the first time was going to be distracting enough for him.

She wanted the man to be able to do that with a clear head.

She was rather surprised that Matt hadn't asked any questions about his daughter yet. After all, the man knew that he was a father. Breena might not have told him, but there had been nothing stopping her, Riley thought, when she had written to Matt. Along with telling him as succinctly as possible that Breena had passed away, Riley had told Matt that he and Breena had a daughter. She'd also mentioned that the little girl was currently residing with Riley's grandfather and her mother, Rita.

Both of them, she recalled fondly, were very good when it came to taking care of the four-year-old, as well as distracting her from the tragedy that she had found herself immersed in.

Nobody wanted the little girl grieving. Instead, what they were attempting to do was to get Vikki to only think about how very lucky she had been to have had Breena as her mother, even for such a short while.

Breena had always been kindhearted and loving. In addition to that, she had always put her daughter's well-being first.

An elementary school teacher, Breena had left Vikki with her best friend's mother when she went to work. Rita Robertson had been more than delighted to look after the little girl.

Rita had continued to look after Vikki until Breena had abruptly stopped working because she'd become too weak and ill to carry on.

Riley found the memory to be stifling and she shook it off.

Breena had been gone for less than two weeks. It was much too soon to deal with that numbing fact right now, Riley thought. She wouldn't be any good at distracting Vikki if she allowed the sadness she was currently managing to hold at bay to swallow her up.

"Do you want to stop at the hotel for a change of clothes?" she suddenly offered, thinking that Matt might want to change into something else before he met his daughter for the first time.

"That might be a little hard," he stated. He saw Riley look at him quizzically. "I haven't checked into the hotel yet. I wanted to stop at Miss Joan's Diner first, to see if she remembered me, or even if the woman was still there," Matt admitted.

The possibility that Miss Joan might have left Forever had struck Riley as amusing.

"Are you kidding? If you want to bet on something that is a sure thing, bet on the fact that Miss Joan is going to go on forever. That woman is never going to retire, or go anywhere else, for that matter," Riley added offhandedly.

For the first time since he had arrived in Forever, Matt caught himself laughing. "When she talked about Miss Joan, I got the distinct impression that Breena thought the woman was immortal," he told Riley. Obviously, he mused, Breena hadn't been alone in that thought.

Riley spared him a glance as they pulled out of the cemetery. "That's because we all think of Miss Joan as being immortal," she informed him with a completely straight face. "Why would you think differently?"

Matt stared at Riley, momentarily speechless. "You are kidding, right?" he asked her. Then, when she didn't answer him, just for good measure, Matt emphasized, "The woman isn't immortal."

Again, she didn't respond immediately. And then, after a beat, Riley kept a straight face as she went on to say, "Until it can be proven otherwise, that's the story about Miss Joan and we're sticking to it. Now, since you haven't checked into the hotel yet, I'm going to take you over to Pop's ranch."

He wasn't comfortable with that. "Shouldn't you

call him instead of just popping up with a stranger in tow?" he asked the woman.

"But I don't have a stranger in tow," she contradicted with a smile. "Pop knows that I'm bringing you over."

Matt's brows furrowed. He was doing his best to try to follow what she was actually saying. "So this was all prearranged?" he asked Riley, waving his hand around the interior of the vehicle as if that was somehow all part of what was going on.

"Yup," Riley answered simply. Judging from her tone, there was no room for an argument.

Even so, Matt found himself rather confused about the whole thing.

Chapter Six

Matt grew very quiet and remained that way for the rest of the trip to Riley's grandfather's ranch house.

At first, Riley had to admit that she was rather grateful for the silence. At least Matt wasn't upbraiding her for something or arguing over the fact that she was taking him somewhere he hadn't said he wanted to go. In all honesty, he hadn't agreed to go to her grandfather's ranch, he just hadn't said that he *didn't* want to go. And he hadn't questioned her about why she was taking him there, seemingly settling for her explanation that her grandfather wanted to meet him.

But she was forced to admit that the continued silence was making her feel increasingly uncomfortable. It was a little like waiting for a pot to unexpectedly suddenly boil over.

Finally, Matt looked in her direction. "Are you sure your grandfather isn't going to be annoyed with having me just pop up in at his house like this?"

"I'm sure." She was about to add that his daughter was also going to be there and that he needed to finally meet her, but she was afraid that saying so might just make him demand to have her turn around and take him back to town. As far as she knew, meeting his daughter was something he needed to do. But Matt could have just put that whole thing out of his mind and ultimately simply forgotten about it.

If that was the case, they could very well wind up arguing about the meeting, and Riley definitely wasn't in the mood to argue with him about that— or about anything else for that matter.

She decided to give him a neutral answer. "My grandfather might look like a gruff man, but trust me, he is a sweetheart, although he wouldn't want to hear me say that. But if he could take being invaded by a pregnant daughter-in-law he didn't even know he'd had in stride, my grandfather can put up with anything."

Riley had managed to catch Matt's attention with that statement. "When was this?" he asked, wanting to know.

She thought for a moment, doing a quick calculation. "That was a little over twenty-six years ago," Riley told him.

Matt gave her a knowing look. "You're referring to yourself," he guessed.

Riley picked up on what wasn't being said. That Breena hadn't mentioned to him that her best friend was one of triplets. But then, why would she have? That summer, Breena and Matt's whole world had revolved around one another, not around her friends.

"Yes," she admitted flatly, "I am."

For only a moment, Riley weighed her options. But there was no real reason to explain that she was one of three. This wasn't about her and she definitely didn't want to take a chance on scaring him off for any reason or even risking making him uncomfortable.

Riley focused on moving forward. "We're almost there now," she relayed. Then, glancing at him, she teased, "Relax, this won't hurt at all."

He had to admit that he was still having trouble understanding why they were going to her grandfather's house to begin with.

"Why would he want to meet me?" Matt, at a loss, was intrigued.

"I told you," Riley repeated. "Pop thought of Breena as another granddaughter."

That made him think about the events that had transpired in the last five years. "Then maybe he'll want to string me up."

Well, at least Matt wasn't looking to charm the man, Riley supposed. "Pop is a very fair man. He'll hear you out first," she promised.

"And *then* he'll string me up," Matt concluded sarcastically.

"Only if he thinks you warrant it," she joked, tongue-in-cheek.

Matt slanted a look at the woman in the driver's seat. "You're not exactly great at calming people's nerves, are you?"

Riley's expression gave nothing away. "I never said I was," she answered.

He sighed, looking forward again. "How much further?" He wanted to know.

She surprised him by saying, "We've been on my grandfather's property for a while now." Then, for his benefit, because she could sense his impatience, she added, "We're almost at the house."

Then Riley pointed to an imposing ranch house in the distance. "In case you don't believe me, it's right there."

Matt looked over to his right toward where she was pointing. The two-story structure was old, but there was something about it, he found himself thinking. Something that, upon closer examination, struck him as imposing and regal. And welcoming.

It had "home" stamped all over it.

Riley pulled up in front of the ranch house and parked her vehicle.

"Remind me never to play poker with you," she told him. He looked at her quizzically. "You have a totally unreadable expression. I can't tell if what you're thinking is good or bad." She gestured to the ranch house, wanting to hear his thoughts about it. "Care to enlighten me?"

Matt didn't answer right away. Instead, he got out of the vehicle slowly, carefully examining the house that was looming in front of him.

"I will," he promised, "as soon as I know myself."

She looked at him as if he had just said something in a foreign language, but decided not to challenge him. At least not yet. For now, Riley allowed him the luxury of getting used to what he was looking at.

Moving in front of him, Riley quickly made her way up the few front steps. Turning back to look at him, she saw that Matt wasn't following her.

"Are you coming?" she quipped, "or are you waiting for your feet to thaw out?"

His forehead wrinkled as he stared at her. "What?"

"That was a veiled reference to you having cold feet," Riley said.

He frowned as he hurried up the steps to join her. "My feet are just fine," he informed her icily.

Rather than get annoyed, she allowed a smile to play along her lips.

That managed to catch his attention. He couldn't help thinking the woman had the kind of smile that easily burrowed into a person's chest and then spread out.

The next moment, Matt forced himself to block the thought. He couldn't afford to be distracted right now.

"So I see," she told him, amused.

Turning in front of the man, Riley stepped up to the tall, imposing double front doors.

He expected her to ring the doorbell. After all, she was bringing a stranger into the house. But instead, she turned the doorknob and just walked in.

"We're here, Pop," she called out, looking around for her grandfather. In the living room.

Within moments, an older man Matt assumed was Riley's grandfather came into the living room. "About time you got here," he told her in a gruff voice. "I was beginning to give up."

A well-built, muscular man of average height, he had a full head of gray hair and a remarkably unlined face, given that he had spent so many years outdoors. Matt caught himself thinking that Riley's grandfather was the kind of man who immediately took charge of any room he entered, even if he didn't say a word.

Magnetic blue eyes immediately pinned his visitor in place. "Hello. Name's Mike Robertson," the older man said by way of introduction as he leaned forward and extended his hand toward Matt.

Matt shook the man's hand. He was surprised at the strong grip.

"Nice to meet you, sir," Matt said. As he took a step back from Riley's grandfather, he became aware of an attractive older woman walking into the room. She flashed a smile at him and he found himself thinking that this had to be Riley's mother.

The woman's smile looked identical to Riley's. The warmth in her eyes made him feel instantly welcomed.

"You must be Matthew," Rita Robertson said, shaking his hand.

"I must be," he replied, thinking that had he known there was this much warmth and friendliness waiting here in this small town, he would have been back a lot sooner—and maybe he might have been able to get through to Breena.

Maybe she might even still be here, he thought sorrowfully.

Matt was about to say something else when he suddenly felt the words abruptly dry up and die on his lips. He found himself stunned by the fact that there were two other young women entering the room. Two young women who, other than the different clothes they were wearing, were completely identical to not just each another, but to Riley, as well.

As he looked from one woman to the other, and then back at Riley, his mouth dropped open. Matt felt like someone who had just stumbled into a dream he couldn't wake up from.

Mike noted the stunned look on the young man's face and chuckled. "I take it that Breena never told you that her best friend was a triplet."

"No, sir, she didn't," Matt admitted, the words all but dribbling from his lips as he looked from one triplet to another and then another. "We didn't spend much time talking about other people—or anything else, really. Triplets," he repeated almost numbly, staring at the young women again.

He had to admit that he had never seen three people look so utterly identical before. It seemed almost uncanny to him.

"How does anyone ever manage to tell you three apart?" He truly wanted to know.

Riley glanced at her sisters, her eyes dancing. She had to admit that she was enjoying this. "Oh, there are ways," Riley told him.

He only knew that it was Riley because he recognized the clothes she was wearing. As for the other two women, he hadn't a clue as to their names or how anyone could manage to tell them apart.

Rita took pity on him and stepped in to make the introductions. "Matthew, I'd like you to meet my other two daughters." She gestured at first one, then the other. "Raegan and Roe—it's really Rosemary, but no one calls her that. It's always been Roe," she declared.

He was doing his best to match the right name to the right person, but even though Rita had made the introductions slowly—and Riley's sisters were wearing different outfits—Matt still found himself confused as to who was who.

So he just nodded at both and murmured, "Pleased to meet you, ladies." Then he looked at Riley and said, "Breena never mentioned that you had two identical sisters."

Riley laughed. "She could be forgiven for that. She might have thought that the idea of triplets might scare you away for some reason," she guessed.

Mike decided to share something personal with

the young man he had just met. "Think how I felt," he said to the young man they had just been introduced to as he continued with his story. "It was a rainy night and there was a knock on my door. In sweeps this fresh-faced, extremely pregnant and rather soggy young woman. I thought she had run out of gas and was looking for help.

"Imagine my surprise when she told me that she was my estranged late son's wife and that she had promised him that if anything ever happened to him, she would come and find me to let me know what had happened. I had no idea that he had joined the military or that he had gotten married—or," Mike said heavily, "that he had been killed in battle saving his men.

"After delivering her message," Mike went on, "my daughter-in-law promptly went into labor."

"Not promptly," Rita corrected her father-in-law with a smile.

Mike carelessly shrugged his shoulders. He wasn't a stickler for details. "Close enough. I was just lucky that Miss Joan had picked that time to come by and check on me." His eyes met Matt's. "The woman was a godsend. She was here to deliver these three," he said, waving his hand at the triplets. "I don't know what I would have done without her.

"The babies just seemed to keep coming and coming," Mike recalled, looking at the threesome fondly. "For a while back there, I didn't think that they would ever stop coming," Mike confided, shaking his head.

"My main regret is that my son Ryan never got to see his daughters." He looked at his guest, his eyes meeting Matt's. "Daughters are a wonderful thing," he told his visitor with sincerity. "Every man should have at least one if possible."

Why did he feel as if he had just been put on notice? Matt wondered uncomfortably.

Chapter Seven

The next moment Matt realized that the woman he thought of as Riley—at this point, only because of the outfit she was wearing—was no longer in the area. He looked around the room but didn't see her anywhere.

He didn't understand.

Had she decided to leave him with her family to fend for himself? It didn't seem like something that she would be inclined to do, but then, he didn't exactly really know her, did he?

Right now, he only saw her two sisters. The remaining triplets were looking at him with the same smile he had seen on Riley's face.

He thought about leaving, but that was not exactly an easy proposition out here, especially since he'd left his car at Miss Joan's diner.

Matt was debating his options when he heard Rita suggest, "Why don't we go into the dining room for that dinner that you were promised?"

With that, the woman hooked her arm through his as she smiled up into his face and led him into the dining room. Her expression mirrored the one that her daughters had flashed.

Matt didn't resist, but the truth was he wasn't exactly sold on the idea of eating with these people without Riley being there.

"Shouldn't we wait for Riley?" he asked, looking at her mother.

But it was Mike who answered him. "She'll be along soon enough." Riley's grandfather tone was intended to assure the younger man. He then winked at him. "Riley's a bright girl. She knows where the dining room is."

She might be bright, Matt thought, but at this point, he would really feel better if she were here. He looked over his shoulder to the doorway that, as far as he knew, led to other parts of the house.

Where is she? he wondered. She hadn't said anything about leaving him to fend for himself. As far as he could tell, the Robertsons were all nice people, but they were still strangers to him and he would have preferred having Riley as a buffer until he knew them a little better.

Rita had brought him over to the end of the table and gestured for him to sit down. Riley's grandfather had made himself comfortable at the head of the table, which Matt assumed was his customary seat.

"Wait for us," Riley called out from the hallway.

A wave of relief washed over Matt. It wasn't until a second later that Riley's words replayed themselves in his head.

Us?

That didn't sound right, Matt thought. Just what did she mean by 'us'? Was there more to her family than just these four people?

He shifted in his seat just in time to look toward the room's entryway to see Riley walking into the dining room.

She was not alone.

Her hand was wrapped around the small, delicate hand belonging to a little girl. As she walked beside Riley, the little girl appeared to be exceedingly shy. Matt noticed that the small child was deliberately avoiding making eye contact with him.

He remembered the letter folded up in his pocket. The letter that had brought him here. The one that Riley had written to notify him about Breena's death and the fact that he had a four-year-old daughter.

For a moment, he had forgotten that last part.

Or maybe thinking about it unsettled him.

Matt's heart stopped as he slowly rose to his feet, staring at the little girl. She appeared to be holding on to Riley's hand for dear life and moving beside her in what seemed like slow motion.

For a second, no one spoke.

And then Mike rose from his chair and moved forward. He smiled down at the little girl. "Hi, kiddo," he said to her by way of a greeting. "Are you hungry?"

Rushing over to stand beside Riley's grandfather, the little girl looked up at Mike and lit up like the proverbial Christmas tree.

"Hi, Pop!" she cried, happy to see the older man, then answered his question. "Yes, sir, I'm hungry."

Her initial hesitant attitude indicated that she sensed this was different from all the other meals she had had at this table. She was still avoiding eye contact with the strange man who was there.

Mike looked at Matt's face, as if trying to gauge just what the man was thinking.

"Matthew Logan, I'd like you to meet Vikki, Breena's daughter." He raised his eyes, pinning Matt in place. For now, he left the rest of the introduction unspoken—that Vikki was his daughter, as well. That part, Mike assumed, would work itself out. For the moment, he'd just said the part of the introduction he'd felt was necessary. "Vikki," Mike continued, "this is Matt Logan. He was a friend of your mom's."

The little girl's eyes lit up when she heard that. For the first time, she smiled broadly at the stranger. "You knew my mommy?" she asked. There was excitement evident in her voice.

"That, he did," Riley said.

Matt fully expected Riley to tell the little girl that he was her father. He braced himself for both the revelation and the way the news would be taken by the child, but neither happened.

Instead, Vikki became animated as a ton of questions seemed to flood into her head.

She came up to him, eagerness resonating in her every word. "Can you tell me about her?" Vikki requested.

Matt felt himself suddenly catapulted in the center of all this. For a second, he was speechless.

Finally, he told the little girl, "I suspect that you probably know much more about her than I do. We hadn't talked to each other for over four years now," he told her, hoping that would satisfy Vikki, at least for the time being.

Vikki looked at him solemnly, as if she were absorbing the information and putting it in its proper place. "I'm four years old," she told him. "That's probably why I don't know about you."

The remark surprised him and he glanced in Riley's direction.

Riley smiled. "I told you that she was smart," she said to Matt. "Tell you what," Riley went on, taking the little girl's hand and leading her over to the table again. "Why don't we have this nice dinner and after we finish eating, your mother's friend can tell us what he remembers about your mom. And then you can tell him what you can remember about her," Riley concluded. "How does that sound?"

The little girl's face was a wreath of smiles. "That sounds really good." Having had the time to digest everything, Vikki looked up at Matt. "I bet I *do* know more stories about my mom than you do."

Matt smiled down at the eager, upturned face. "I bet you do, too," he told her. "And you can tell me some of them after we finish eating."

Vikki's eyes shone as she grinned at the man sitting at one end of the table. Like the rest of the family, he was treating her as if she were a small adult, not a little kid. That made her happy and it also made her want to be that small adult.

"I will," she promised.

Riley exchanged a pleased look with her grandfather. "Looks to me like Vikki likes him," she observed in a low voice.

"Why shouldn't she?" Raegan asked. "Her mother obviously did."

Matt looked a little embarrassed and then he glanced at the woman who had just spoken. For the life of him, he didn't know which triplet she was. "You ladies really should come with name tags," he commented.

"I'm Raegan," the woman who had just spoken told him.

Matt's eyes shifted over to the last of the triplets. "Which means that you are—"

"Roe," she announced, inclining her head in his direction.

Matt slowly looked from one triplet to the other and then toward the one who was wearing Riley's outfit. Giving up, he sighed, shaking his head. "No, there is no way I am going to ever manage to tell the three of you apart," he said.

"Oh, sure you are," Mike countered. "Here, I'll get you started," he offered. "Riley talks faster than her sisters. She's also a darn fine nurse." He'd clearly amended "damn" to "darn" at the last moment because Vikki was seated at the table with them.

"Raegan is a problem solver. There are times when you can almost 'see' her thinking. And, Roe... well, she is a vet and has an affinity for animals. She always has. You hang around her long enough and you can almost see the animals sensing that. It's not something that you notice at first glance," Mike confided, "but at second and third glance...well, it really starts to come to the surface. It goes without saying that the girls are all good with animals, but not like Roe. The talents they have influence the way that you see the girls." And then the family patriarch paused and cleared his throat. "Or should I be saying 'young women'?" he asked, looking from one to the other to the third. It was a genuine question on his part.

Riley spoke up before the others. "Pop, we'll always be your 'girls' even when we turn a hundred."

Mike laughed. "At that point, I will just be a pile of old rotting bones laying somewhere," he told his granddaughters.

"Oh, Pop." Raegan waved a hand at the man. "You know you are never going to grow old, much less die and leave us."

The older man made a dismissive noise that

sounded like "humph." It was followed by words to that effect. "From your lips to God's ears—as long as you girls promise to pick me up every time I wind up falling down."

Matt sat back, taking all of this in and thinking that there was a great deal of love generated within this family unit.

One of the few things he had known about Breena was that she had been an orphan, and he sincerely hoped that she had been able to find the love that she had initially been missing, here amid this close-knit family. He had the feeling that she probably had.

"Don't worry, Pop. I'll be there to pick you up," Vikki promised, looking at him with all the seriousness of a four-going-on-thirty-year-old.

Mike laughed. Leaning over, he tousled the little girl's silky red hair. "I knew I could count on you, sweetheart," he said affectionately.

Vikki nodded her head with all the solemnity of someone a great deal older making the pledge. "Always, Pop."

That caused everyone to laugh. Rosa picked that moment to walk in, carrying a tray that had the main course—pot roast, mashed potatoes, peas and carrots—swimming in a large bowl of gravy.

Despite the fact he had thought that he wasn't hungry, the tempting scent got to Matt almost immediately. "That does smell good," he said as Rosa placed the bowl in the center of the table and then withdrew.

For a moment, no one made a move. And then Vikki spoke up.

"You're the guest," she told the man sitting at the other end of the table. "So you get to go first. You use the big spoon in the bowl." Her hint was offered in what could be referred to as a stage voice.

"That's a ladle," Ripley reminded the little girl helpfully.

Vikki nodded. "Right," she agreed. "You use the ladle," Vikki told Matt authoritatively, oblivious to the fact that the people she knew were trying their best to hide the wide, amused grins that rose to their lips as she explained protocol at the table. "That way, you can put more food into your own bowl."

Matt had never made it a point to hang around children, although some of his friends were parents and he did occasionally cross paths with their offspring. But to his knowledge, none of them sounded nearly as intelligent as Vikki did.

"How old did you say she was?" he asked, looking at Riley. He knew that in the letter he'd received from Riley, she had said Vikki was four, but that didn't really seem possible. She sounded so much older.

Before Riley could answer, Vikki piped up, "I'm four and two months." The little girl held up four fingers to emphasize the fact.

Matt shook his head in amazement. "You have to be the brightest four-year-old I've ever met."

Vikki looked at him with wide eyes and was not shy about asking what she wanted to know. "How many have you met?" The question completely threw him for a loop.

It took Matt a second to restrain the laugh that rose to his lips. The last thing he wanted was to make Vikki think that he was laughing at her.

But it definitely was not easy.

Chapter Eight

"I think that had to be the best pot roast that I've ever had," Matt said, moving his chair back from the dining table. Without thinking, he momentarily rested his hands on his stomach. "I think I might even be too full to get up and walk."

Mike laughed. "Well, nobody's planning on chasing you away from the table. If I were you, I'd just let the food settle."

"Time for bed, young lady," Rita told Vikki.

The little girl looked disappointed. "Aw, do I have to go to bed now?" she asked. She looked from Riley's mother to Riley and then she looked at Matt, obviously trying to determine who her best bet was when it came to staying up late.

Rita did her best to look stern, although she didn't

quite succeed. She hadn't been able to get the hang of looking stern even when her daughters were little.

"It's important for you to get enough sleep, sweetie," she told Vikki.

The sad look on the child's face moved him. He could remember resisting being sent off to bed at her age. "Maybe she can get a little more sleep on the other end of the cycle," Matt suggested.

Vikki looked ready to jump up and down in agreement even though it was obvious that she really didn't understand what he was saying.

"Yes, please," she said, looking from one person to another at the table, appealing to all five of them.

Riley turned toward Matt. "Don't look now," she whispered to him, "but I think you just became Vikki's new hero."

Managing to overhear Riley, the little girl vigorously nodded her head up and down. "Uh-huh," she said.

Matt couldn't help laughing. "I can live with that," he told Riley.

"All right," Rita reluctantly agreed, temporarily giving in. "But just for another half hour. After that, it's off to bed with you, little one. No ifs, ands, or buts," Mike's daughter-in-law informed the little girl.

Vikki vigorously nodded her head. "No ifs, ands, or buts," she repeated, smiling. And then she went on to shyly ask, "Can Matt be the one who puts me to bed?"

The question caught him completely off guard. At a loss, he looked to Riley for guidance.

There was something obviously there between Matt and his daughter, even though the connection hadn't been noted out loud, Riley thought.

Very subtly, Breena's best friend nodded her head, letting Matt know that it was all right for him to agree to the terms that Vikki had just laid out.

"I'd be happy to," Matt said. "But I don't know where your room is."

Or even, he realized, if she actually had one in the ranch house. After all, it wasn't as if she had lived here all that long, he thought.

"I can show you," the little girl volunteered eagerly. "Pop said that we came here so much that he wanted us to have a room of our own so we could feel welcome." She beamed from ear to ear.

"'We'?" Matt questioned, not sure if he understood what she was saying.

"My mama and me," Vikki answered. For a second, her expression became very serious and Matt was afraid she was going to start to cry. But the next moment, the little girl's bright smile was back.

Reaching up, she took his hand and wrapped her small fingers around one of his. She tugged on it, indicating that he should follow her.

Matt looked over his shoulder at Riley, his silent message crystal-clear.

Come with me, his eyes requested.

Riley was quick to pick up on that, happy that the

little girl had taken to the man so quickly. She just hoped that the feeling was reciprocated.

Meanwhile, Vikki was happily leading her mother's friend to what she now thought of as "her" room.

It was located on the second floor at the end of the hall; a small room, perfect for someone of Vikki's size.

Peering in, Matt had a hard time visualizing Breena staying there with the little girl, but then, from what he knew of Breena's childhood, the room's size was something she would have grown into, he judged. He knew that Breena hadn't required much and, once again, he regretted that things had turned out the way they had.

But then, if he hadn't been able to be there for Breena—or their daughter—he was glad that she had found a friend like Riley. He could tell that Riley and her family provided the kind of support and backing that Breena had obviously needed and thrived on.

If only—

Matt shut down his mind. There was no sense in going there, he told himself.

"This is my room," Vikki announced proudly, gesturing around.

Matt nodded. "It looks like a very nice room," he told his daughter.

The little girl bounced onto the bed then looked up at him, all eager smiles. "Would you like to try it out?" she asked.

He pretended to think about it then said, "Maybe

some other time. Right now, I think you should be getting ready for bed."

Vikki looked up at him, all smiles. "Okay, I will." With that, Vikki began to undress.

Unprepared for what was happening, Matt turned away and looked toward Riley for help.

A wide, amused smile blossomed on her lips as Riley tried not to laugh. "Okay, little one, let's get you ready for bed," she said. Looking at Matt, she said, "Why don't you get Vikki's pajamas out of that drawer?"

When he just stared at her, lost, Riley nodded at a child-sized chest of drawers against the wall, just beside the small bed specially made for the little girl by Pop, who'd found carpentry to be very relaxing.

When Matt opened the top drawer as directed, he found several sets of pajamas neatly folded and in different colors. He pretended to consider the various pairs. "Okay, would you like a blue pair, or a pink pair or a green pair?" he asked the little girl, turning to look at her.

It was obvious that she liked being consulted and paused to think before saying, "The blue pair, please."

Matt nodded, taking the pajamas out. "That would be my choice, too," he told her. "Blue is my favorite color." Handing the pajamas to Riley, he swiveled and kept his eyes averted.

Within moments, Vikki piped up, "It's okay to look now. I'm all dressed."

Nonetheless, Matt turned around slowly in her direction, just in case she wasn't as "all dressed" as she thought she was.

But her pajamas were on.

"So you are," he noted with approval.

Vikki scrambled onto her bed and was about to pull her covers up over her body when Riley gave her a look. "Vikki, didn't you forget something?"

The light suddenly came into the girl's eyes. "Oh, yeah, I forgot to say my prayers," she said.

She got out of bed and knelt down on the floor beside it. Folding her hands before her, she began to recite, "Now I lay me down to sleep, I pray the Lord my soul to keep. Bless my mama in heaven. Bless Pop and Grandma Rita, and Aunt Riley and Aunt Raegan and Aunt Roe." Vikki snuck a look in Matt's direction. "And bless my mama's friend. I just wish she could have been here to see him."

Matt hadn't expected her words to affect him as much as they had. He could feel their resonance in his chest and moisture gathering in the corners of his eyes.

And then Vikki added words that he'd never, ever, anticipated hearing.

"And bless my daddy, wherever he is. Amen!" she announced. Finished, Vikki crossed herself and burrowed into her bed, pulling the covers up to her chin.

Matt cleared his throat. "Well, good night," he said to the little girl.

Instead of saying the words back to him the way

he thought she would, Vikki asked, "Can you tell me a story? Just a little one," she added, looking at him hopefully. She created a small space between her thumb and pointer finger to show just how little a story she was requesting.

He, in turn, looked at Riley, a helpless expression on his face. "I don't know any stories," he admitted helplessly.

"Sure you do," Riley told him. "Everybody knows at least one story if not more. I'll even start you off."

Sitting on the edge of Vikki's bed, she began, "Once upon a time there were three bears. A papa bear, a mama bear and a little bitty baby bear. And there was a girl named Goldilocks…"

Pausing, Riley looked at Matt. "Okay, take it away," she encouraged. When he didn't say anything, she gave him an incredulous look. "C'mon, you've got to know the story of 'Goldilocks and the Three Bears,'" she said.

He was aware of it, but not much more. "I heard it a long time ago," he told her.

"That's okay," Vikki said, urging, "Just tell us what you remember."

He sighed, thinking. "Well, Goldilocks came into the house…" he said, at a loss as to how to continue.

"And the three bears were out," Riley prompted Matt helpfully.

"Right, the three bears were out. They were taking a walk," he said, guessing. He was rewarded with a wide smile from Riley.

"Good. And then what happened?" she asked, prompting, "Was Goldilocks hungry?"

"Right," Matt answered, grasping at the crumb she had thrown his way. "Goldilocks was hungry."

"And?" Riley asked him.

He felt two sets of eyes on him as he resumed. "And she found some food in the refrigerator, so she ate it," he declared triumphantly. Belatedly, he turned to Vikki. "She ate what was in the refrigerator," he repeated.

"Right," Riley said. Then, prompting when Matt didn't say anything immediately, "And then what happened? Did she get tired?"

"Oh, yeah. She got tired—so she lay down," he told his small audience, continuing with the narrative.

"And she promptly fell asleep," Riley added, filling in.

Matt nodded. "Right," he agreed. "She promptly fell asleep."

"And then what happened?" Riley asked, a smile playing on her lips.

"I know, I know," Vikki cried, waving her hand as if she was waiting to be called upon.

"Okay, Vikki, you tell Matt what happened," Riley said.

"The three bears came home. The Papa Bear said, 'Someone has been eating our food,'" Vikki said in as deep a voice as she could manage.

Riley nodded. "And what else?" She urged the little girl to continue.

"Mama Bear said, 'Someone's been playing with my clothes and they scattered them all about,'" Vikki said solemnly.

Riley inclined her head as she suppressed a grin. "Close enough. And then what happened?"

When Vikki looked up at her quizzically, Riley asked her, "What did the Baby Bear say?"

Vikki thought for a minute then grinned as she declared, "'Someone's been sleeping in my bed and there she is!' And then Goldilocks opened her eyes, saw the three bears standing around her, and jumped out of the bed. She ran all the way home and never went exploring any more. The end," Vikki declared, very pleased with herself.

Riley inclined her head. "Again," she declared with a laugh, "close enough."

Vikki stifled a yawn. "Can I have another story?" she asked.

"Tomorrow, pumpkin," Riley told her, pulling up the covers. "Not today."

A protest rose to the little girl's lips, but it wasn't really strong enough to make it out. Her eyes were fluttering and, after one or two attempts to keep them open, Vikki gave up and let her lids close.

The even breathing that followed shortly thereafter told them that Vikki was asleep.

Riley looked at the man sitting across from her on the other side of the bed.

"Congratulations," she declared. "You just made it through your first bedtime story in what I gather was probably a very long time. How do you feel?" she asked Matt.

"Honestly?"

"Yes," she answered. Why would she want him to lie?

"Drained," he admitted.

"It'll get better," she promised.

The expression on his face told her that he had his doubts about that.

Chapter Nine

"You're welcome to stay the night," Mike told his guest as Riley and Matt returned to the dining room after Vikki fell asleep.

Matt shook his head. "That's all right, sir. I wouldn't want to put you out," he told the older man.

"Who said anything about being put out?" Mike asked. "We've got lots of room here at the ranch and this will give you a chance to get to know Vikki a little better, right, Rita?" he asked, smiling at his daughter-in-law. Ever since Rita had come into his life, Mike found that his sad, lonely, dark world had become a great deal happier and brighter. That went three times as much because of the girls.

"Still, I think I should check into the hotel. I'll

be back in the morning, if that's all right with you?" Matt said, looking at the older man.

"That'll be fine with me," Mike assured him. "I still think that that's a lot of trouble to go through in order to wind up in the same place tomorrow morning." Still, he was not about to argue with Vikki's father. He looked at the granddaughter closest to him. "Riley, would you mind running this stubborn guy into town?"

"Actually, I was planning on going into town to check on a patient I treated. I can drop Vikki's dad off at the same time," Riley told her grandfather.

Her statement caught Matt's attention. "That sounds like you pretty much have a full-time job. What did you say you did for a living?" he asked Riley.

"I'm a nurse practitioner," she replied. "As a matter of fact, I delivered your daughter. Breena went into labor extremely fast. She was early and there was no time to get her to the hospital," Riley recalled. She remembered the events as if they had taken place yesterday.

"Breena gave birth to Vikki just before breakfast," Riley told him. "That was my trial by fire," she admitted fondly. Her mouth curved deeply as she relived the experience. "Scariest thing I ever went through."

Mike lifted the single glass of wine he allowed himself to imbibe every evening, toasting Riley. "And you came through it with flying colors." He congratulated his granddaughter then glanced in

Matt's direction and said proudly, "All my girls are a credit to their chosen professions."

Matt realized that his education was sorely deficient when it came to Breena's friends. He hadn't known any of their names, much less what any of them did for a living. It was time to fix that.

"What are your professions?" Matt was curious. "I realize that you said you were a nurse practitioner, but as for your sisters…" His voice trailed off as he shrugged and waited to be filled in, at least by one of them.

Riley's glance swept over her sisters before she told Matt, "Raegan is an engineer. She helped build the dam and replenished the town's water supply during the last drought that we had here." Riley's voice was filled with pride. "And Roe is a veterinarian. That's self-explanatory," she added with a wide grin.

"I guess you're not resting on your laurels," Matt commented, impressed.

Riley looked at him, feigning surprise. "Where's the fun in that?" she quipped. "We country girls like to earn our own way," Riley told Vikki's father.

"Admirable," he returned in all seriousness.

"Practical," Riley corrected. She couldn't imagine what it was like, doing absolutely nothing, not earning her own way. At least to some degree.

Matt was not about to argue semantics. Instead, he just shrugged. "Have it your way," he said.

Mike laughed, amused. "If you stick around here long enough, you'll find that she usually does," he told his guest, then added for good measure, "All my girls are very stubborn, including their mother. They get that from their grandmother—even Rita." Mike glanced at his watch. "You'd better be on your way if you want to make good time and check on that patient of yours," he told Riley, "and get back here at a decent hour."

"Right as usual, Pop," Riley said.

Roe brushed her lips against Mike's cheek, as did Raegan. "We'd better get going, too, Pop. I promised Alan I'd be home early. He just got back into town after working on a project for the past month."

Mike nodded, taking the information in. "Next time, have him come along, too," he told Raegan. "I haven't seen your husband for a while."

"Me, neither," Raegan said with a laugh. "Seems like he's been away, working, more than he's been home lately. He needs to work a little less," she commented.

Mike nodded. "Like I said, bring him along next time." And then he looked at their guest. "And you're welcome here, as well, for as long as you're in town," he told Vikki's father. "We don't stand on ceremony or formality around here." The man smiled at Matt. "It was nice to see Vikki smiling again," he added. "That little girl hasn't done that since her mama died."

The reference to Breena's death weighed heavily on Matt. No matter which way he viewed it, he just couldn't forgive himself for never being able to get

Breena to come around to his way of thinking. He should have somehow been able to plead his case and convince Breena to answer him.

Maybe if he had returned to Forever sooner and made his case in person instead of just giving in to Breena, thinking she had fallen for someone else, he could have won her over.

"Don't take this the wrong way," Rita said, walking up to Matt. "But how long are you planning on staying in our town?"

Riley smirked, shaking her head. Leave it to her mother. "Here's your hat, sir," she said in a formal, teasing voice, "what's your hurry?"

And then she laughed out loud as her eyes met Vikki's father's, hoping she hadn't insulted him.

"I'm not sure yet," Matt admitted seriously, thinking the question over. "That all depends on how things wind up going."

Riley inclined her head. Time to wrap this up, she thought. Her eyes slid over his handsome features, doing her best not to react. "Are you ready to go?"

"Any time you're ready," he answered.

"Ready," Riley declared with a wide smile.

Her grandfather chuckled. "Doesn't leave you guessing, does she?"

"Actually, I find that a rather reassuring quality," Matt admitted. He hadn't noticed the smile that had slipped over Riley's face.

Following Riley to the door, Matt paused to shake hands with the people who had welcomed him into their home. Mike had been especially warm and hearty.

"I had a really nice time," he said to both Mike and Mike's daughter-in-law. "And would you tell Rosa that I really enjoyed the dinner she made?"

Mike nodded, more than happy to oblige the man's request. "I'm sure that Rosa already knows that—there's nothing wrong with that woman's ego or her hearing. But between all of us, she'll be pleased to know that you said that." Mike clapped the young man on the shoulder. "Don't be a stranger," he told Matt, then looked at Riley. "Get home safe."

"Not to worry, Pop. I fully intend to."

With that, Riley led the way out the front door. Matt was quick to follow.

"I'll take you to the hotel first," she offered.

"You can just let me off in the general vicinity and I can walk to the hotel," Matt told her.

"For that matter, I can just let you off here and you can walk all the way." Riley tried to hold a straight face before she laughed off his suggestion. "Don't be ridiculous, I'm driving you there," she informed him firmly. "You look tired," she pointed out. "I can just pick up your suitcase and take you to the hotel. No arguing," she underscored. "You won't win."

She waited a few minutes as the silence in the car grew more pronounced. Then, finally, she asked Matt, "Well, what did you think?"

He turned his head toward her, not exactly sure

what she was asking. "Of what?" He wanted to be certain he understood.

Riley sighed. "Of the world situation," she said sarcastically, "and if there's going to be another world war." She added with a somewhat impatient sigh, "Of Vikki, of course."

He thought for a moment. "She acts older than I thought she would," Matt answered honestly, turning his eyes back to the road in front of them.

Riley laughed. "The standing joke for all of us was that we thought that Vikki acted like a little old lady from the day she was born. Now that you've met her," Riley said, getting back to her original question, "what are your plans?" She wanted to know.

That caught him a little off guard. "To be honest, I really don't have any plans just yet. I'm just getting used to the idea of actually *having* a daughter," he admitted.

As far as Matt was concerned, this was all brandnew to him. He hadn't even thought about having children down the line, much less about having a daughter now.

Riley nodded her head as she continued driving. "Fair enough."

In all honesty, she really wasn't sure just how she wanted this to go. She didn't like the idea of having Vikki move away so she could go live with her father, but then again, that was not her decision to make. What she wanted didn't matter all that much in this case. She recalled that Breena had wanted Vikki to be with her father. Why else would her best friend have asked her to write to Matt to let him know that she had died, that he had a daughter to raise and care for?

In all honesty, with Breena gone, Riley had thought of Vikki as belonging to her and to her family. Thinking of the little girl as Matt's daughter would take some adjusting, Riley couldn't help admitting to herself.

"First things first," Riley announced. "Let's get you a room at the hotel," she told the engineer. "Once you're settled in and get a good night's sleep, we can tackle tomorrow."

He had to admit that he was rather tired and saw no reason to disagree with what Riley was proposing. As he sat back, Riley guided her vehicle into the hotel's front parking lot. Getting as close to the revolving front door as possible, she parked, pulling up the handbrake.

"Don't forget to get your suitcase out of the trunk," she reminded Matt as she got out of the driver's side.

"Thanks," he told her as he got out on his side then nodded toward the trunk of her car. "Just pop it open for me."

Riley smiled, picking up on his tone. "I had a feeling you'd remember," she told him. "But you did have a long day today as well as a long drive," she reminded him. "You could have easily forgotten to take your suitcase with you."

After all, the man had met his daughter for the

first time, met Breena's friends, and dealt with the memory of the woman he had been in love with and thought he had lost, not to mention having to go through Miss Joan's interrogation. That would have been more than enough to make any man lose his train of thought.

Matt picked up his suitcase and took it with him as he followed behind Riley into the hotel. He looked around the lobby, taking it all in. "They did some renovations since I was here last," he noted.

"Good eye." Riley nodded. "That comes from never being satisfied." She chuckled and then smiled at him as they walked up to the front desk. "If you're not moving forward, you're standing still, or worse, sliding backward," she gibed.

There was no one at the front desk. Stopping, Matt looked at her and laughed quietly, acknowledging her remark. "My father would have liked you."

"'Would have'?" she questioned.

Matt nodded. "He died last year,"

"I'm sorry to hear that," she said sympathetically. "I guess that gives us something in common, although it would be nicer to have something else in common instead."

Matt raised his brow quizzically at her comment, waiting for her to fill him in. "Meaning?"

"My dad died, too. He was killed while in the army, just before my sisters and I were ever born," she told him. "That's why my mother came out to find my grandfather. My dad told her that if anything should ever happen to him, she should come out here and look my grandfather up—which is rather odd when you think about it."

Matt wasn't following her. "How so?" He wanted to understand.

"Well, my father and grandfather never really got along and they had a huge falling out after my grandmother died. They just couldn't bring themselves to exchange so much as a civil word. Both of them really missed having my grandmother around. From what I gathered, my grandmother was their peacemaker.

"Eventually, unable to go on butting heads with my grandfather, my father finally enlisted in the army. That's where he met and married my mom." She paused for a moment before continuing. "With time, he had a change of heart about my grandfather. He became calmer and forgave my grandfather even though he never got in touch with Pop. He always figured there would be time enough for that later.

"When my mother found herself expecting triplets, my dad was overseas and he *really* had a change of heart. He worried a lot about her being alone, so he made her promise to find his dad just in case anything ever happened to him while he was fighting overseas."

"And something did happen to him," Matt concluded, watching her expression.

Riley nodded. She could finally say the words without having them hurt. It had taken a long time to reach that stage. "It did. So she came out here and the rest, as they say," she concluded, "is history."

Matt nodded. "I get that," he said just as the hotel clerk came out of the back room to register him.

Chapter Ten

That had gone well, Riley thought after she left the medical clinic and finally began the drive back to the ranch house.

She was thinking about the way her day had gone, not about her quick nighttime pit stop to see her patient at the clinic.

As far as the latter went, she had been just in time to see Dr. Davenport, the last doctor there, about to lock up and leave for the evening.

"Go home, Riley," the doctor had told her. "For once, there's nothing for you to pack up or put away. I checked Jane and am happy to say that she's doing even better than we expected. I sent her home. Where you should be," Davenport added.

Riley had lost no time in taking the doctor up on his suggestion.

As she drove, her mind couldn't help but gravitate to Matt. Although the word "daddy" hadn't been mentioned, Vikki had seemed to adjust rather nicely to Matt and he to her, Riley thought with a satisfied smile.

"You were right, Breena," Riley said aloud to the memory of her best friend. "He really did turn out to be a nice guy."

Not to mention handsome, she thought. She could see why Breena had fallen for Matt. There was something magnetic about the man; something that, if she allowed it, could easily pull her in.

And that meant she just couldn't allow that to happen, she sternly warned herself.

It was still hard for Riley to adjust to the fact that Breena was never going to walk into her house again, never share anything in confidence.

Never laugh with her again.

The very thought made her heart hurt.

Riley blinked back tears.

Everyone in her family—for that matter, everyone in town, as well—loved Breena. But she had loved Breena most of all. And, with the exception of Vikki, she was the one who missed her friend the most.

She still hadn't made up her mind how she felt about the idea of Matt taking custody of Vikki, if that meant taking her back to Arizona, which is probable. The possibility hadn't been discussed one way or the other.

But it would be.

"All in good time, Riley," Riley cautioned herself. She just might be getting ahead of herself. For all she knew, Matt was just visiting, curious to see what this daughter of his looked like. He might not even be thinking of taking her back with him. After all, that wasn't just a big step, it was a huge commitment. A permanent one.

For that matter, Vikki might not want to go with him. And if moving away wound up generating tears for the little girl, then Riley intended to do everything in her power to put a deterrent in the man's way and keep Vikki here with everyone she knew and loved.

However, that might not even be necessary, Riley realized. When she'd caught Matt looking at Vikki, he'd struck her as someone who was deeply out of his element.

Riley blew out a breath. What was she worried about? she asked herself. In all probability, Matt would be on his way home after this visit of his was over.

As she pulled up to the front of the house, Riley saw that the lights were still on. True to form, her grandfather was waiting up for her. He always did when he knew that she was staying over.

Riley unlocked the door. Sure enough, her grandfather was sitting in his chair. The paper he had been reading was slipping off his lap and he appeared to be in the process of dozing off.

The moment she closed the door behind her, despite the fact that she was trying not to make a sound, her grandfather's head jerked up.

Blinking, he cleared his throat and asked, "Did you manage to get Matt a room at the hotel?"

"I didn't have to, Pop," she told him, stepping out of her shoes. "He got his own room."

Mike frowned. "You know what I mean, little girl," he told Riley.

She grinned in response. "Yes, I do," she confirmed. "Luckily for me, I speak 'Pop.'"

Mike chuckled. "Well, after all these years, I would certainly hope so," he told his granddaughter.

"So, Riley," he then said, getting down to business, "what do you think of this guy Matt?"

"I don't know yet." She answered honestly. "It all depends on whether or not he takes Vikki away with him or leaves her here."

Despite the fact that he had his own opinion on the matter, Mike asked, "Which way are you leaning?"

Her eyes met his. "Honestly?"

"I'd expect nothing less from you or from your sisters," he told her. Lying was not a habit that any of the triplets had ever indulged in. He saw no reason for them to begin now.

"I'd want Matt to find a way to stay here with Vikki," she said. "It would be a lot easier on her. And the rest of us."

Listening to Riley, her grandfather nodded. "One big happy family?" he suggested.

That did sound rather naïve, Riley thought. Still, it was what she would prefer. "Something like that." Heading for the stairs, she sighed, admitting, "This would have more of chance of working if Breena was still here with us."

"And you would have more of a chance of working if you went to bed and got some rest before you have to go in," her grandfather told her.

As usual, he was right, she mused. "Raegan and Roe go home?"

"Did you see either one of their cars outside?" Mike asked her.

She flushed. "No. That was a silly question on my part." Taking a couple of steps up, she paused, saying, "Thanks for making Matt feel welcomed." She was speaking for Breena.

He looked surprised that she felt she had to express gratitude. Mike came up to her. "He's Vikki's father. Throwing rocks at the man wasn't exactly part of the deal," her grandfather told her.

Coming down a step, her eyes laughing at him, Riley brushed her lips against her grandfather's cheek. "You do realize that those jokes of yours are all rather outdated, right?"

He laughed and then shrugged. "I'm waiting for a comeback."

"Don't hold your breath, Pop," she advised. "I'd hate to see you pass out."

Mike laughed again, louder this time. "That's my girl," he said. "Always thinking of me."

Her eyes smiled at him. "Always. Good night, Pop."

Riley was exhausted as she went up to her room, but for the most part, sleep took a long time in coming. It insisted on playing hide-and-seek for a good portion of the night.

But she finally managed to drift off just a little before morning.

Out of the goodness of his heart, Dan Davenport, the doctor who had hired her and whom she thought of as her boss, had insisted that she take the next few days off to spend with Vikki and her father.

The offer, coming from out of nowhere last night, had surprised her. "Aren't you going to need me?" she'd asked.

From experience, she'd known how swamped the clinic could get and, although they now had more people working on the premises than they used to, she'd also known that the clinic could still get super crowded as well as super busy.

"It'll be hard," the doctor had told her. "But barring an out-and-out emergency, we'll find a way to do without you for a week." He'd looked at her seriously. "This is important to you as well as to Vikki."

She'd been tired, but not too tired to express her gratitude. "Have I told you how much I like working for you, Dr. Davenport?"

"Not this week, but it's still early," he'd told her. "Feel free to say so any time you want."

"I will." Riley had pretended to clear her throat, adding an enthusiastic, "You really are great."

The doctor had merely chuckled. "I just might call on you to serve as a character witness the next time my wife gets annoyed over the hours that I'm forced to keep away from home."

Riley had been grinning as she had left the clinic that night. "Consider me to be your character-wit-ness-in-chief," she'd told him.

This morning, as she came to the hotel to pick Matt up to bring him to the ranch, she found herself having to pass by the clinic. A wave of guilt washed over her. She knew that the doctors who worked at the clinic would have been the first to take her to task for feeling guilty, but she couldn't help it.

She had always experienced a huge sense of ob-ligation when it came to her work, despite what the doctor had told her.

For a second, she was tempted to peek into the front window and double-check that no emergency had come up since last night or early this morn-ing. But she knew that there were enough people on duty at the clinic to handle anything that might have come up.

Once upon a time, there had only been one doctor in town, and that had been after a lengthy "drought." A second doctor had come along not all that long afterward. And then a third. The nurses, including herself, soon followed. And that was before the hospital had been built.

"Your ego is getting the better of you," Riley said to herself as she resisted temptation and kept her eyes on the road. "They would have called you if they had needed you. Everything is under control. The world does not revolve exclusively around you."

With that, she focused on driving toward the hotel. She turned up the radio, using the music to drown out any miscellaneous thoughts that were attempting to crowd into her head.

Parking her vehicle in the hotel's parking lot a few minutes later, she made her way through the lobby. As she did so, it occurred to Riley that she didn't know if Matt was an early riser or if he liked to sleep in. After all, he wasn't a rancher where getting up before the crack of dawn or thereabouts was required, or came naturally to him.

Well, no time like the present to find out, Riley thought. At least Vikki would be awake by the time she brought Matt to the house. She had heard the little girl stirring as she'd headed downstairs, but Vikki was still not up when she had left for town.

Riley recognized the woman at the front desk. Paige Billingsley was someone she had grown up with as well as attended elementary school with. During those years, she recalled Paige had told anyone who would listen that her life's ambition was to become a model. But then Paige had fallen in love with Mark Nelson and all those carefully cherished plans had just gone out the window. Paige and Mark had married a little more than a year ago.

"Hi, Paige," Riley greeted the young woman as she reached the front desk.

For her part, Paige looked really surprised to see Riley. "Hi. Did someone call the clinic, saying they were sick?" she asked, jumping to the most logical conclusion.

"No, I'm here to pick up one of the guests who's staying at your hotel," Riley informed her former school friend.

Paige glanced at the computer screen where all the current guests who were checked in were listed. There was never that many people staying at the hotel at any one time, but as news of the new hotel in Forever spread it was now doing a respectable amount of business, depending on the season.

The look in Paige's brown eyes reflected her interest as she glanced up at her.

Riley was quick to answer the unspoken question she saw there. "He checked in last night," she added.

"Name?" Paige asked even as her index finger slid down the column of guests.

"Matthew Logan."

"Friend of yours?" Paige asked, her curiosity getting the better of her.

Ever since Paige had gotten married to Mark, she seemed devoted to the idea that everyone she knew had to be paired up with someone, if not actually married to them.

"He was a friend of Breena's," Riley told the hotel clerk.

At the mention of Riley's late best friend's name, pity filled Paige's eyes. "I was really sorry to hear about what happened to Breen," she said with total sincerity.

"We all were," Riley said, hoping the woman would drop the subject. "Could you tell me what room he's in?"

"Give me a second," Paige told her, skimming the names on the screen once again in earnest. And then her face lit up. "Ah, here he is. Matthew Logan. He's staying in Room 310," she announced. "He checked in last night," she added as if that was news. She glanced up at Riley. "Want me to ring his room for you?"

"Thanks, but that won't be necessary." Riley answered, already walking away. "I can take the elevator up to his room."

And then she proceeded to do just that.

Chapter Eleven

There was someone knocking on his door.

Matt groaned. Maybe if he didn't make any attempt to answer, whoever was on the other side of the door would take the hint and go away.

It felt as if he had just closed his eyes and had finally fallen asleep. He was definitely not ready to face the day. Although, he congratulated himself, he had made it through yesterday pretty much intact. But he was not all that optimistic about successfully going for day number two.

He made no effort to get up. Most likely, he thought lazily, it was complimentary room service. He knew he hadn't placed an order for anything.

The knocking came again. This time it sounded louder and more urgent. Whoever was on the other side of that door was not going to go away, Matt resolved with a weary sigh.

"Keep your shirt on," he said, swinging his legs off the mattress and onto the floor. He padded barefoot over to the door. "I'm coming. I'm coming," he called to the person who was knocking.

"Good," Riley said the second that Matt opened the door. "Because I was going to keep on knocking until you let me in."

Matt blew out a breath. He should have known, he mused, opening the door wider. He waited for Riley to cross the threshold. Once she did, he closed and locked the door behind her.

"Tell me, when did you realize that you were such a shrinking violet?" he asked her, having trouble keeping a straight face.

Riley never missed a beat. "Probably around the same time it occurred to you that you had the kind of silver tongue that could charm the birds right out of the trees," she answered innocently.

Matt inclined his head, a hint of a smile playing on his lips. "Touché."

"Shall we go back to our corners and start over again?" she asked.

Matt nodded. "Sounds as good a plan as any," he told her. And then he looked at her thoughtfully, his own words replaying themselves in his head. They hadn't really talked about anything beyond checking into the hotel. "Just what do you have planned for today?"

Her eyes swept over him. He was wearing the hotel bathrobe and she had a feeling that he had nothing on underneath. She didn't allow her thoughts to go any further. "Well, to begin with," she said, "I think that you should get dressed."

Matt glanced down. He'd forgotten what he had on. "You don't need to tell me that. I wasn't planning on streaking."

"Good, because the sheriff frowns on things like that happening, and you wouldn't want to get arrested your second day here," she told him glibly.

"No, I'm saving that for my third or maybe fourth day," he gibed, deadpan.

"Speaking of which," Riley began, picking up on what he was saying.

Matt raised one eyebrow. Where was she going with this? "Yes?"

"How long do you plan on being here?"

That was an odd thing to ask him, he thought. "Why? Do you plan on running me out on a rail?"

She gave him an odd look. "Quite the contrary. I was hoping that you would be here for at least a few days. I thought it might take that long for you and Vikki to adjust to one another."

He thought that he and the little girl were doing just fine the way they were. Had he missed something here? Matt continued looking at her for a moment longer, doing his best to guess what was on Riley's mind.

"And then what?" He wanted to know where this was leading.

Riley shrugged her shoulders. "And then we'll see," she concluded philosophically. "She is your daughter, but that doesn't automatically mean that you can just pick up your relationship from there and live happily ever after. In case it escaped you, this is a very delicate situation that you have just found yourself in."

In response, Matt laughed dryly. She was not telling him anything he hadn't already thought of himself. "No kidding, Sherlock," he quipped.

Her eyebrows drew together. "It wouldn't hurt to park that attitude of yours somewhere," she chided.

For a second, he felt himself growing defensive, and then he realized that she was right. Uncomfortable situations always put him on his guard.

"This would have been a lot easier all around, five years ago," Matt said more to himself than to Riley.

"Everything would have been a lot easier five years ago," she told him. "But life doesn't always follow a blueprint, no matter how much we might want it to."

"Amen to that," he murmured.

She had a feeling that they were talking about the same thing, but she wasn't about to press him on that.

"So, if there's nothing else, I'm going to take my shower," he said, tightening the bathrobe around himself.

"Go right ahead," she said, gesturing toward the small bathroom.

He paused for just a moment, an amused smile playing on his lips. "And if I need help scrubbing my back?"

For a second, Riley could feel herself growing warm, but she never hesitated. "I can put a call in to Pop, but you might have to wait a while," she told him, just the slightest trace of humor playing on her lips.

He liked the fact that she didn't rattle easily. "Not necessary," he told her. "I can manage."

Matt could see that her eyes were laughing at him and he found himself smiling. He was beginning to see why Riley and Breena had gotten along so well.

Riley inclined her head, acknowledging his remark. "I'm sure you can," she told him. She gestured once again at the bathroom door. "I'll just wait out here."

"I'll try to be quick," he told her.

What she said stopped him in his tracks for a second. "Don't just 'try,'" she intoned. "Be."

Matt paused just before he entered the bathroom, one hand on the doorknob. "Do you order your patients around, too?" he asked, looking back at her over his shoulder.

He saw the mirth in her eyes.

"Actually, yes, I do," she answered. "That's how I wound up perfecting my technique."

He couldn't exactly explain just why, but her response really tickled him. "I should have guessed," he said.

Riley liked the way that he took things in stride. She was beginning to really understand what Breena had seen in him. He wasn't just easy on the eyes, she liked his approach to things.

She decided that it was only fair to share something with him. "My sisters would tell you that I take some getting used to."

Matt caught himself thinking that truer words had probably never been spoken. With that, he grabbed a fresh set of clothes and went to take a quick shower.

He was out within less than ten minutes. "Done," he needlessly announced.

Riley turned around to face him. She couldn't help thinking that the man really was as fast as he thought he was.

"Your hair's wet," she noted.

"I was afraid that you'd take off without me if you thought I was taking too long," he told her, tossing his wet towel into the small, boxlike hamper.

Why would he think that? she wondered. "I'm not that impatient," Riley told him.

The expression in his eyes made it clear that he thought differently. But he was not about to contest the matter.

Matt wasn't looking to get into any sort of an argument with her, certainly not this early in the day. For now, he intended to be on his best behavior. He needed all the allies he could get as he felt his way around in this unknown area known as "fatherhood."

"Sorry," he apologized. "My mistake," he said as he tucked his shirt into his waistband.

She felt as if they were dancing around something, but in all honesty, she really couldn't say just what that was. For now, it was simply safer for her to withdraw from any verbal sparring match, not to mention easier.

"Apology accepted," Riley told him. Her eyes washed over him as she thought of a more basic, pertinent question to put to him, although she was fairly certain she already knew what his answer would be. "Have you had breakfast, or at least coffee, yet?" Riley wanted to take the "fairly" out of the "certain."

She was kidding, right? "I was half asleep when you knocked on my door," Matt pointed out. "What do you think?"

Her mouth curved. "I think you need to pay a visit to Miss Joan's before we make the trip back to Pop's ranch. Vikki is usually full of energy first thing in the morning, so you are definitely going to need your strength if you intend to keep up."

But he saw a problem with stopping to eat at the diner. "Your grandfather, not to mention Vikki, might not take kindly to being kept waiting."

"Trust me, having breakfast at Miss Joan's is a good investment," she assured him. "And Pop and Vikki will understand."

Matt wasn't convinced but he shrugged his shoulders. "If you say so."

They rode down in the elevator together and Riley led the way through the lobby. She was keenly aware of the fact that Paige was still stationed at the front desk and that the woman was watching every step both Riley and the handsome hotel guest with her made.

A look of deep appreciation entered the hotel clerk's eyes as she observed the duo heading for the revolving door. It was obvious the woman really liked what she saw.

"I see you found him," Paige called out.

Riley glanced in Matt's direction before telling the woman, "He was just where he was supposed to be." She flashed Vikki's dad a pleased smile.

In response, Matt raised a quizzical eyebrow. "Was I missing?" he asked Riley, slightly bewildered.

"Not that I know of." Seeing the question in Matt's eyes, Riley lowered her voice as they went through the revolving door and said, "I know her from high school," she explained. "This is the perfect job for her. Paige always liked to keep tabs on *everyone*. She still does," Riley added just as they walked outside the hotel.

She headed toward where she had left her vehicle in the parking lot.

Riley pressed the button on her key fob to simultaneously unlock all the doors. Matt obliged by getting in on the passenger side and then buckling up.

As Riley started up her vehicle, Matt began to have second thoughts about their initial destination. He put his hand on her wrist. It was meant to stop her, but Riley looked at him quizzically.

"Did you forget something?" she asked.

"No, but you really don't have to go to the diner," Matt told her.

"Oh?" she asked. "Why not?" Riley got the impression that Matt really needed some coffee to get his motor going—and having some breakfast wouldn't exactly hurt, either. She had the feeling that he wasn't one of those people who did well when he was hungry.

"I don't want to keep Vikki waiting," he said, repeating his earlier excuse.

Riley flashed a warm smile at him. "That's really very nice of you," she told him. "But Vikki isn't one of those impatient little kids who wants to know what time it is every couple of minutes. She is actually accustomed to waiting." Riley went on. "And as for you, I actually think you will be better off grabbing at least a little something to eat. It'll keep you from getting grumpy."

His eyes narrowed. Had she just insulted him? "I don't get grumpy," he informed her.

"*Everyone* gets grumpy when they're hungry," Riley countered.

"Even you?" he asked.

She greeted his question with a laugh. "Yes, even me," she answered.

Matt thought of another deterrent. Remembering something that Breena had told him about Miss Joan, he said, "If Miss Joan sees us together, she's liable to have endless questions to fire at me—at us," he corrected.

She was well aware of the way Miss Joan operated. "I know," she said innocently.

"Then why would we go?" he challenged. Riley wasn't making any sense, he thought.

For as long as she could remember, the owner of the diner had always been one of her favorite people. Not to mention that Miss Joan was the one who'd delivered Riley and her sisters. From the things that Riley had managed to piece together once she had become a nurse, her mother might have died in childbirth if it hadn't been for Miss Joan. But for now, she would tell Matt just what she was feeling. "Because I wouldn't dream of denying Miss Joan one of her few pleasures in life," Riley stated very honestly.

The expression on Matt's face didn't exactly say that he shared her opinion on the matter. Still, he sighed and nodded his head.

"All right, if it means that much to you, we can go."

Amusement played on Riley's lips.

"Thank you," she said, inclining her head. "Just so you know, breakfast is on me."

Chapter Twelve

As was her habit, the moment she heard someone coming in, Miss Joan's eyes darted over to the door. When she saw who it was, she automatically poured two cups of coffee, one black, one with cream, and brought the cups over to place them side by side on the counter.

"You're still here," she noted, a trace of surprise echoing in her voice. The words were directed toward Matt.

"I am," he acknowledged. "Takes a while to get to know someone," he explained, referring to Vikki. He had made no decisions about the girl's future yet, but he wasn't about to be hasty when it came to making that decision.

In the meantime, Miss Joan's hazel eyes pointedly

washed over Riley as she agreed with Matt's obser-
vation. "That, it does."

Surprised by the silent implication she saw in
the woman's eyes, Riley thought Miss Joan had the
wrong idea.

Or maybe she didn't, Riley realized the next moment. Maybe Miss Joan was intimating that Matt was
checking her out, thinking of her as his daughter's
potential guardian.

Now that she thought about it, Riley decided, that
didn't seem nearly as farfetched as she might have
initially believed.

"We're here for breakfast," Riley told the older
woman.

Miss Joan laughed shortly. "And here I thought
you came here for the scintillating conversation."
She placed a menu in front of Matt and then looked
at Riley. "I don't figure I have to give you a menu.
Nothing's changed since you were a little girl."

"Nothing?" Matt questioned in surprise.

Miss Joan shrugged. "When you've got something
good going, why mess with success?" she asked,
looking at the young man sitting at her counter.

Matt rolled the question over in his head. "Well,
for one thing, tastes can change," he told Miss Joan.

"We're very basic people around here," Miss Joan
said by way of explanation. "We usually like eating
the same things we've eaten before."

To emphasize her point, the owner of the diner
looked pointedly at the coffee Matt had in front
of him.

Time to move this along, Riley thought.

"Speaking of which," Riley said, deciding to make Matt's choice for him, "we'll have two breakfast specials." She went on to specify two scrambled eggs, four slices of bacon and two slices of rye toast. Finished, she looked at Matt. "Unless you'd like something else instead?"

Miss Joan pinned the man sitting beside Riley with a look. "Would you?"

Matt couldn't help thinking that the way Miss Joan had just worded her question was actually more of a challenge than anything else. He had no intention of beginning the day on the wrong side of this woman. Besides, food was food, and he had never been that fussy an eater.

"No, what Riley had just selected will do nicely," he told Miss Joan, then added for clarity, "Anything that's quick." The diner owner was about to comment on his request when Matt explained, "I don't want to keep Vikki or Mr. Robertson waiting."

Miss Joan's eyes narrowed and she looked at him for a long moment, as if debating whether or not what Matt had said was on the level. She decided to give him the benefit of the doubt.

With a bob of her head, the woman gave Matt a half smile and said, "You know, kid, you're not half bad at that."

Matt was a little taken aback, not sure if she was pulling his leg or if she was being serious. Because of that, his "Thank you" sounded just a little uncertain.

Turning toward the young woman who was in charge of preparing breakfasts in the small kitchen, Miss Joan ordered Riley and Matt's breakfasts. "Two specials, Virginia. And make it quick." She nodded at Matt and Riley. "These people are in a hurry."

"Yes, ma'am," Virginia answered, promptly disappearing into the recesses of the little kitchen.

"But don't sacrifice the taste," Miss Joan warned, raising her voice so that it would follow after the short-order cook.

"No, ma'am," Virginia called out.

Miss Joan turned back to look at Riley and the young man next to her. "Breakfast will be right out," she promised.

Matt glanced at his watch. He didn't say anything, but it was obvious he was prepared to wait for a while.

The engineer was clearly surprised that, by the time he had taken a few sips of his coffee, breakfast had been brought out and placed in front of him.

"She wasn't kidding, was she?" he sighed, somewhat marveled as he looked at Riley.

"Miss Joan never kids," Riley assured him just before she took her first bite of her scrambled eggs.

For his part, Matt made short work of consuming his breakfast. Consequently, he was finished well before Riley was.

The latter gave him a quizzical look. "Did you even bother chewing before you swallowed?" She wanted to know.

"I chewed," Matt protested.

Riley gave him a skeptical look. She didn't believe him. "Uh-huh." But she couldn't really fault him, not when she knew that he was in a hurry because he didn't want to keep his daughter waiting.

Riley automatically picked up her pace.

Matt watched her in silence for a moment before finally telling Riley, "Just because I'm finished doesn't mean that you have to eat fast."

She gave him a side-eye as she quickly consumed what was left on her plate. "Yes it does," she told him, then added, "I have always been very competitive. Just ask my sisters."

"I'll take your word for it," he said. There was no need to take the matter any further.

Leaning forward in his seat, Matt dug out his wallet.

Riley caught the movement out of the corner of her eye. "Put it away," she ordered him. "I already told you that breakfast was on me."

"I am not about to be a kept man," he informed her, a hint of a smile on his lips as he rose from the counter stool and stood up.

"You're both wrong," Miss Joan informed them, making her way over to the duo. "Breakfast was on me." She saw the challenging look that Matt gave her. "Consider it your reward for sticking it out," she told him.

His being in Forever had nothing to do with the owner of the diner. "But I can't—"

Miss Joan turned to Riley. "Did you tell this young man that no one ever gives me an argument?" Her tone made it clear that she wanted to know.

Riley was about to answer when Matt asked Miss Joan incredulously, "No one?"

He didn't think that was actually possible, but then, he did come from a city that was a great deal bigger than this small Texas town.

Miss Joan considered her initial answer and decided to amend it. "Well, no one who's ever lived," the woman responded. Her look darkened as she glared down at the wallet Matt was still holding open. "I'd put that away if you ever want to use that hand again."

Matt was beginning to learn when he needed to drop an argument. This was one of those times. "Well, I guess that you just sold me."

There was a smile in Miss Joan's eyes if not actually on her lips. "I thought I might."

The diner owner reached under the counter and took out a bag filled with what looked to be a fresh batch of chocolate-chip cookies, placing it on the counter in front of Matt.

"Give that little girl a big hug from me," Miss Joan said. "And also these." She opened the bag for a moment. A warm scent wafted up, swirling around them as it filled the air to the point that it made their mouths water. "Those are for her, not for you," Miss Joan informed them authoritatively. "If she chooses to share her cookies with you...well, that's up to her.

But don't just presume that she will. If you do, trust me, I will know." The woman's eyes met Matt's, a very serious expression on her face.

Matt backed off. He smiled as he nodded at the older woman. "I wouldn't dream of it, Miss Joan," he said in all seriousness. He looked in Riley's direction. "Let's go," he prompted. "I don't want to keep Vikki waiting."

And then, just before he started to follow Riley, he took out a twenty and placed it on the counter.

"I thought I told you breakfast was on me—" Miss Joan began sharply.

"You did. This is for Victoria. Best breakfast I've ever had," he said in all sincerity, silently apologizing to his mother since he knew that his compliment didn't exactly cast her in the best kind of light. But then, his mother had a lot of other saving graces that clearly set her apart.

Miss Joan pressed her lips together as she regarded the twenty on the counter. "All right, I'll pass on your comment," she told Matt. "And the twenty."

He smiled at the diner owner. "I'd appreciate it," he said by way of thanks.

Riley was clearly impressed as they walked out of the diner. "I think that's the fastest I've ever seen Miss Joan warm up to anyone," she told Matt as they walked out into the diner's parking lot.

"You think she's warming up to me?" he asked Riley, surprised. Miss Joan was not the easiest person to read, he thought.

"Oh, I know she is," Riley assured him with more than a degree of certainty.

He was still rather mystified. "How can you tell?" Matt asked.

"Well, for one thing, when she looks at you, her eyes are not shooting daggers. I noticed that there was even a half smile at the end there. She really likes the fact that you're making an effort to be part of Vikki's life."

"Well, I can't just ignore her," he pointed out. "After all, she is my daughter."

Riley stopped at her vehicle and opened her door, waiting for Matt to do the same on the passenger side before getting in. "You would be surprised to find out how many men *don't* think that way. You know 'out of sight, out of mind.' That sort of thing."

"Well, that's not my sort of thing," he told Riley, distancing himself from that notion. Getting into the vehicle, he huffed as his mind went back. "That first year when Breena didn't answer any of my emails or my texts, not to mention my phone calls, I didn't know what to think. We parted on such good terms, and then nothing," he said with a helpless, confused sigh. "If I hadn't been so tied up with that last year of schoolwork, trying to get my degree, I would have been back out here in a heartbeat.

"But there were classes I needed to catch up on and things that still needed doing, so I couldn't just drop everything to come back. Part of me, at the time, was convinced that I was doing all this not just for me, but for Breena, too." In his mind's eye, he could envision it all.

"But the more time that passed, the more convinced I was that I was lying to myself. That what we had, at least in Breena's opinion, was nothing more than a summer romance, one she had recovered from and then moved on. So, after dozens of letters—none of which she ever answered, probably never even opened—I told myself that I was beating my head against the wall and it was getting me nowhere—except for giving me a hell of a headache. So I gave up and did my best to move on, although I have to admit that there was a part of me that kept hoping that maybe if I backed off, Breena would wind up changing her mind.

"But she didn't," he concluded sadly.

"No, she didn't," Riley told him. "She didn't change her mind when it came to you. She always loved you," she emphasized.

"Right," he said sarcastically. "That's why she never answered any of my letters, never got in contact with me at all."

"Exactly," Riley confirmed. She could feel him looking at her. "She wanted you to feel free, not to feel tied down in a situation where you felt obligated to take care of her and her child."

Matt stared at Riley's profile, stunned. He had never looked at it that way. "You're serious."

Lifting one hand off the wheel, Riley went through the motions of crossing her heart. "Completely."

Sparing him a look to see how he was taking all this, she said, "I'm like Miss Joan. I never lie."

Matt really wanted to believe her, but he felt it was too soon.

Still, he desperately wanted to be convinced.

Chapter Thirteen

Vikki shifted from one foot to another as she continued standing guard by the front window. She had been standing there, looking out the window and watching every movement that occurred at the front of the house. She had been doing that from the moment she had finished eating breakfast and been excused from the kitchen table.

She didn't seem to get tired, Mike marveled, watching the little girl.

"Why don't you come back here and sit down?" Riley's grandfather suggested, not for the first time. "I promise I'll call you the minute that Riley arrives with Mr. Logan," he told the little girl.

Vikki continued staring out the window, waiting.

"You mean with my daddy, right?" she corrected the older man whom she thought of as her grandfather.

Mike paused, exchanging looks with his daughter-in-law. To his knowledge, no one had referred to the man Riley had brought into his home as Vikki's father. For some reason, the little girl had just seemed to infer that that was his identity.

How?

He decided to press the matter. "Who told you he was your daddy, honey?"

Turning from the window just for a second, Vikki raised her eyes upward a little, as if seeing something that he couldn't.

"Mama did," she answered, then went back to looking out the window and keeping vigil.

As far as Mike and his daughter-in-law knew, Breena had never showed her daughter a picture of Matt, never said anything about his being her father.

"When did she tell you that?" Mike couldn't help asking the child.

The look on Vikki's face was innocence personified. "Yesterday," the little girl answered.

Breena had been gone for a little more than a week, but Vikki's answer had been adamant, even as she continued standing guard by the window.

Mike and his daughter-in-law fell silent for a moment in the face of Vikki's fierce reply. After a beat, Riley's mother opened her mouth to dispute the little girl's answer, but Mike placed his hand on top of Rita's, stopping her.

She looked at her father-in-law, raising her eyebrows in a silent query.

"Who are we to dispute what Vikki believes to be true?" he asked quietly.

Suddenly, Vikki stood at attention, her entire small body becoming rigid as she stared out the window, her eyes widening.

"He's here!" she cried excitedly. "He's here!" Shifting so that she had better access to the door, Vikki began attempting to pull it open.

"Vikki," Rita asked, coming forward to join her father-in-law and the child at the door, "what did we tell you about the front door?"

Vikki's expression fell just a little as she froze, her small shoulders raised in a shrug. "You said not to open it," she replied morosely.

"Right," Mike agreed. "And what is it that you're doing right now?" He wanted her to understand.

Vikki looked down at the tips of her shoes. "Trying to open it," she confessed.

"As long as we're clear on the concept," Mike told her. It earned him a confused, puckered scowl from Vikki. The little girl clearly didn't understand. "What I'm saying is that you understand what you're trying to do is wrong," he explained.

"Oooohhhh." Vikki stretched the word out as the meaning of what Riley's grandfather was saying to her suddenly became much clearer.

Just then, Vikki picked up on the sound of the

front door being opened. She spun around on her heel to face it in time to see it happening.

Her face lit up. "They're here!" she cried happily, then further clarified, *"He's* here!"

Vikki quickly cut the distance between herself and the front door as she dashed toward it, all but bouncing up and down at the same time.

"You're here!" she cried excitedly.

Vikki hardly waited for Matt to walk in with Riley. Instead, she wrapped her arms around the part of her father she could reach, which in this case turned out to be one of his legs. She had what amounted to almost a stranglehold on it, squeezing it as hard as she could.

Bending over, slipping his arm around his daughter, Matt looked over to Riley. He was at a complete loss for words.

Riley found herself responding to the warm, happy expression on Vikki's face. "He couldn't wait to come back to see you," she told the little girl, then added, "And he brought you something."

"What?" Vikki wanted to know, eagerly shifting from foot to foot. "What did you bring me?"

For a second, overwhelmed by Vikki's greeting and her question, Matt temporarily drew a blank. And then he saw that the little girl was looking at the bag he was still holding. The one that Miss Joan had given him as they'd left the diner.

"Oh, right." Matt nodded, upbraiding himself for his momentary memory lapse. Clearing his throat, he asked, "Vikki, how do you feel about chocolate-chip cookies?"

"I *love* chocolate-chip cookies," the little girl cried with enthusiasm. Then, almost shyly she asked him, eyes widening, "Do you have any chocolate-chip cookies with you?"

"I might," he said casually.

Matt found he could barely contain the smile that rose to his lips. With effort, he looked down at the bag Miss Joan had given him. Holding it up, he shook it gently near his ear, as if he was trying to guess what the bag's contents might be.

"Uh-oh, what's this?" he asked Vikki, looking at her for input.

"Chocolate-chip cookies?" Vikki cried hopefully, her eyes curious.

Watching the exchange between Matt and his daughter, Riley felt her heart swelling. She knew that this scene that was playing itself out at the moment would have made Breena very happy.

"Hmm. Why don't we open up the bag and see what it is?" Matt suggested.

Vikki clapped her hands together as if to encourage the man she now regarded as her father to do exactly that: open the bag.

Matt played up the moment. With slow, deliberate movements, he dramatically opened up the bag he had been holding. He made a production out of looking into the bag—and then he abruptly closed it again.

"What is it? What is it?" Vikki cried excitedly, shifting from foot to foot and waiting for Matt to answer her.

Matt looked into Vikki's bright little face. "Guess," he challenged her.

Vikki sucked in her breath for a second, then, eyes dancing, she asked, "Is it chocolate-chip cookies?"

The grin on Matt's face momentarily shifted. "Aw, you guessed."

With that, he handed the bag over to her, slanting a look at Riley to confirm that he was ultimately doing the right thing. Matt would have been the first one to confirm that he wasn't accustomed to dealing with children and wasn't sure just how to act around them, even an intelligent child like Vikki.

Vikki happily all but snatched the bag of cookies from him.

Matt was concerned that he might have misjudged the girl. Looking at Riley, he lowered his voice and asked, "She's not the kind of kid who'll eat cookies until she's ready to explode, is she?" Matt fervently hoped that he hadn't made a mistake in judgment.

Instead of answering his question directly, Riley nodded at the little girl and quietly said, "Just watch."

Holding the cookie bag in front of her, Vikki had presented herself in front of Riley's grandfather and offered it to him. "Want a few cookies, Pop?" she asked.

Mike Robertson pretended to think his answer over, looked into the bag's contents and then said,

"Thank you, Vikki. I don't mind if I do." With that, he took one cookie out of the bag.

Vikki repeated the process with Riley's mother, with her father, and, finally, she held the bag up for Riley to accept a cookie. Only then did the little girl indulge her own craving for a chocolate-chip cookie.

Observing her, Matt could only marvel at the self-restraint Vikki had demonstrated. He inclined his head toward Riley, dropping his voice once again. "If I hadn't seen it, I wouldn't have believed it. She's an incredible little girl."

"That is all Breena's doing," Riley told him. "Without being harsh or overly strict, she had been molding Vikki from the time she was a little baby," she informed Vikki's father proudly.

"She's not exaggerating," Rita told the young man, coming up to join them. "I have no idea how she did it, but I certainly wish I had had her gift when I was raising my own little gang," she said.

"Go easy on yourself, Rita. You didn't exactly raise an all-female version of Bonnie and Clyde," Mike said, coming to his daughter-in-law's defense. "I'm sure that if my son is looking down right now, he's smiling at the job that you've managed to do.

"Heck," Mike laughed, "he might even be moved to say something nice about me." Mike had thrown that last part in, recalling that things had definitely not been on the best footing when he and his only son had parted company.

Matt smiled. "Maybe it's the drinking water here," he said with a philosophical smile.

"Why would the water make someone do something?" Vikki asked, confused, her brow furrowing.

"It's just a joke, honey," Riley told her, pulling her closer to give her a hug.

"Oh." And then the little redhead proceeded to laugh, as if her funny bone had been tickled.

Riley hugged the child even closer. "She picks up cues really well," she told Matt, then went on to tell Vikki with feeling, "Sometimes I think that I could just eat you all up."

The little girl looked at her with extremely wide eyes. It was obvious that Vikki was having trouble reconciling what had just been said with the fact that she really liked her mother's friend, but really didn't want to be eaten by her.

This time, Matt was the one to come to Vikki's rescue.

Repeating the words Riley had previously used to assure Vikki that what he had said about the water was really just a joke, Matt told her solemnly, "It's a joke, honey."

But this time, Vikki looked as if she didn't know if she was supposed to laugh or not. Her large eyes searched the faces of the four people who were around her.

"I've got an idea, Vikki," Riley quickly interjected. "Just eat the chocolate-chip cookies. We all know that they're really tasty."

"Do they make them that way?" Vikki asked, curious as she took another big bite.

"Miss Joan made these cookies and she always makes sure that they're super tasty," Riley told the little girl.

"Miss Joan," Vikki repeated thoughtfully. It was obvious that she was trying to connect the name to a face. "Is that the lady with the red hair and the pretty brown eyes?"

Riley could only laugh and shake her head. She was going to have to remember to tell Miss Joan that.

"You have got some memory, little girl," she said to Vikki. As a nurse, Riley dealt with a number of children, but she couldn't recall encountering any as sharp as Vikki was. "When you grow up, you are definitely going to give people a run for their money." She grinned at the child.

"Why would I do that?" Vikki asked her mother's friend. No sooner were the words out of her mouth than her head bobbed up and down. "Oh, I know. That's another joke, right?" she asked, her eyes growing large as she looked at Riley for confirmation.

Riley was careful not to say anything that could be misunderstood or taken cryptically. She just bobbed her head and assured the little girl. "You're absolutely right, honey."

Vikki was peering thoughtfully into the bag she was holding. "There's only one cookie left," she said as she looked at the others in the room, torn as to what she should do.

"Why don't you eat it?" Matt suggested.

But Vikki shook her head. "That wouldn't be right. Mama told me not to be greedy. Mama was always right." And with that, Vikki took the last cookie and broke it into four pieces, then she distributed the four pieces between the four adults sitting with her. The pieces were accompanied by a wide smile.

"But where's your piece, honey?" Rita asked.

"I don't need a piece. I'm full," Vikki declared, patting her stomach for emphasis as she grinned. "See?"

Chapter Fourteen

Matt was amazed at how well his visit with Vikki was going. Every day held something new. Thanks to Riley's suggestion, he, his daughter and Riley went on a picnic near the lake a couple of days later. Rosa had been recruited to pack a picnic basket filled with pieces of crisp, fried chicken, a large sealed container of french fries as well as a package of freshly baked brownies and a large thermos of punch.

"That smells really good," Mike had commented the moment that Rosa had placed the picnic basket on the table. The air had immediately filled with the delectable scent of the newly prepared meal.

Riley had never hesitated in extending the invitation, assuming that Matt would welcome the company. It would help to take the pressure off Matt.

"You're welcome to come with us, Pop," she'd told her grandfather.

"Yeah, come," Vikki had echoed, her bright eyes shining.

Not wanting to be conspicuously left out of the communal invitation, Matt had added his own voice: "What they said," he'd told the man at the head of the table with a smile, nodding in the direction of his daughter and Riley.

"Thanks," Mike had said, responding to the invitation as he envisioned taking part in the picnic they were proposing. "But I'm afraid that my days spent on the ground, crouching on my knees, are over."

Vikki, Matt had begun to learn, was not one who readily accepted failure the first time around. "You can bring a chair, or sit on a big, bouncy cushion, Pop," she'd told the man.

Mike had laughed, ruffling Vikki's hair. "No, that's all right, honey. You three deserve to have a picnic by yourselves. Maybe we can all go on a picnic together some other time. I know that your sisters would welcome the break, as well," he had said, looking at Riley. "But for now…" Mike's voice had trailed off, his meaning clear.

Riley had conceded with, "Understood, Pop," then turned her eyes to the other two people at the table. "Well, Matt, I believe we're being given the bum's rush."

"We are?" Vikki'd asked, her expression reflecting her utter confusion. "What's that?" She'd been clearly mystified.

She was going to have to choose her words more carefully around Vikki, Riley had thought. "It's an expression, sweetie."

"I know that," Vikki had said with a touch of impatience. "But what does it mean?"

"It means I'm going to have to be more careful about the things I say," Riley had explained with a sigh.

Matt had decided to step in to try to smooth out the situation. "Back in the very old days, some people weren't very kind when it came to poor people. They referred to those poor people as 'bums' and when they wanted to get rid of them, they called it 'the bum's rush' and would run them out of town." He had responded to the look of concern on his daughter's face. "They don't do that anymore," Matt had told her.

"I'm glad," Vikki had declared. "That doesn't sound that they were being very nice."

Matt had caught himself beaming at his daughter—it was getting easier and easier for him to think of her in that light.

"They weren't," he'd agreed, then said to Riley, "Okay, so it's just going to be the three of us then?" He wanted to know for certain.

Riley had looked at her mother and her grandfather one last time. Neither had looked as if they would contradict that assumption, so she had nodded confirmation. "It looks that way." And then she had declared, "Okay, people, let's go."

Riley had started to move to retrieve the picnic basket, only to be edged out of the way.

Matt had wound up picking up the basket himself. "Let's go," he'd echoed, gesturing for her to lead the way out of the house.

Beaming, Vikki had gleefully followed, pausing only to turn around and wave madly at Pop and Rita before she'd rushed out to Riley's vehicle.

The car had been parked in its usual spot, which was on the far side of the driveway. Vikki hadn't had to be told what to do. She had immediately gotten into the back of the vehicle and proceeded to wiggle into the car seat. The latter was secured directly behind the front passenger seat, allowing Riley to glance back at the little girl to make sure that everything was all right every few feet if she needed to.

Riley had strapped Vikki in, ensuring that all the straps were secure and that there was no chance of Vikki undoing anything. She was taking no chances that the little girl could endanger herself, or accidentally go flying if the vehicle had to make a sudden stop.

She'd noted that Matt had been watching the child's every move. She'd liked that. Liked the fact that he was being conscientious and attentive to Vikki.

Apparently, she'd thought to herself, she had misjudged the man. This was definitely not the end of the line for him, she'd decided, and so far, he was making a very decent showing when it came to fatherhood.

Riley had highly approved.

It was a beautiful, sunny day and the closer they came to the lake, the more excited Vikki grew.

"I take it that she doesn't get to go to the lake very often," Matt guessed, looking toward Riley for confirmation.

"Well, not recently," Riley replied. Her tone told him that Breena hadn't been able to do too much because of her increasingly weakening state.

Matt decided not to pursue the matter any further at the moment. The subject was too close to the fact that Breena had grown progressively weaker over time. If nothing else, talking about the matter could easily upset Vikki and the point of this picnic was to get the little girl to smile, not to make her sad or morose.

Suddenly, Vikki seemed to come to life. "There it is!" she announced excitedly as she pointed at the water. Then, in case there was any doubt, she declared, "It's the lake!"

Matt laughed warmly. "That it is," he agreed. "There's certainly no fooling you, is there?"

She moved her head from side to side, solemnly answering his question. "No, there isn't."

Riley stopped her vehicle, parking it in a clearly accessible place.

"Everybody out," she declared, twisting around in her seat and looking at Vikki to make sure the little girl heard. "Matt, will you do the honors?" she asked.

Matt got out of the car and made his way to the back. Approaching Vikki's car seat, he looked a little uncertain. Trying to undo the buckles, he was at first confounded. But by the time Riley had made her way around to his side, he was successful and beamed at her triumphantly as the belts snapped apart.

"Very good." Riley congratulated Vikki's father as he helped the little girl wiggle out of the car seat.

Vikki landed on the ground with a small thud then grabbed hold of his hand, clutching it firmly in both hands as she smiled up at him.

Holding on to Vikki's hand with one hand, Matt took hold of the picnic basket with the other and then made a judgment call.

"You get to bring the blanket," he told Riley.

Watching Matt with Vikki, Riley liked what she was seeing. They really seemed to be getting along. She grinned as she retrieved the blanket. Holding it against her, she followed behind Matt and Vikki.

"I'm not sure I can handle it, but I'll try," she told him whimsically.

Vikki twisted around to look at her. "You can do it," she cried, earnestly encouraging Riley.

Riley pressed her lips together, doing her best not to laugh. She didn't want to take a chance on hurting the little girl's feelings.

"Would you like to pick out a spot for us?" Matt asked his daughter.

Vikki nodded intently. But she stopped walking a good distance away from the shoreline.

"How about here?" she asked, gesturing around.

Matt looked somewhat surprised. It was pretty far from the edge of the lake. "Wouldn't you like to get a little closer to the water?" he asked Vikki.

"No." The answer was flat and uttered without any fanfare.

Matt didn't want to seem like he was challenging the little girl, but she had definitely aroused his curiosity. "Why not?"

"Mama always said not to get too close to the water," Vikki explained solemnly. "I could drown."

He saw the look that came over Riley's face, as if something had suddenly dawned on her. He leaned in closer so only she could hear his question. "What is it?" he asked, wanting to be enlightened.

"When Breena was a little girl, she almost drowned. She had to be rescued out of the lake and given mouth to mouth. She never went swimming after that, making up one excuse after the other until people just stopped asking her. They let her have her space when it came to swimming. I never made the connection, but now that I look back, she never let Vikki go swimming," she revealed.

"I really think that she should learn how to swim," Matt told Riley as he and Vikki spread out the blanket. "Kids run the risk of drowning," he said quietly.

"If she gets swimming lessons, that'll make one less thing to worry about," he concluded seriously, slanting a look in his daughter's direction.

"You're right," Riley agreed. "But that's a discussion for another time," she told him. "Right now—" she smiled brightly at Vikki "—I think we should go ahead and have our picnic."

The child's eyes lit up. It was easy to see, Matt thought, that Vikki loved socializing and doing things.

"Yes, please," the little girl said.

Riley looked at her and very seriously asked, "Vikki, would you like to help me put the food out for the picnic?"

The small red head bobbed up and down as Vikki patiently waited to receive her instructions.

Grinning at her, Riley pulled out three large plastic plates and three smaller plastic plates, and the paper napkins that were set down next to them on the blanket. She also took out the various covered bowls, removed the covers and made sure that the bowls were reachable from all sides.

Riley looked at the small, solemn face that had been watching her every move and asked, "Would you like to put out the forks and spoons? They need to go on top of the napkins."

"Oh, yes," she cried with glee, as if she had just been asked to do something really spectacular.

Riley absolutely loved the little girl's enthusiasm, as did, she would be willing to bet, Matt. She gestured toward the picnic basket. "Then go right ahead," Riley encouraged Vikki.

Matt looked on, silently impressed by how capable this small human being already seemed to be. Recalling some of his friends' children, although he'd seldom paid much attention to them to any real degree, he was convinced that he had never run into even one who'd seemed nearly as capable or self-assured as this four-year-old.

And he didn't think of Vikki in those terms because she was his daughter. He had never been that vain or competitive. Hell, he had never even thought about having children. Children were something that other people had. Quite honestly, when he looked back, fatherhood had not been on his agenda.

But having found himself suddenly catapulted into that position, he was forced to view the whole process through very different eyes.

Through no fault—or planning—of her own, this little jewel was his daughter and he realized that he couldn't have hoped for a more perfect human being to fit that part.

The only question that remained, he thought, and it was a big one, was just where did Vikki and he go from here?

Try as he might to figure it out, Matt realized that he had no answer.

Yet.

Chapter Fifteen

"You know, I didn't think it was possible, but I think we actually tired her out," Matt said. He was carrying the little girl in his arms. Vikki was sound asleep.

It had been a day filled with games, exploring the area around the lake, taking in the scenery and eating. Consequently, long before sundown came, Vikki was clearly exhausted. But she'd kept denying it even as her small eyes were closing.

Riley laughed in response to his comment. "She certainly went down fighting," the nurse practitioner confirmed. Her eyes swept over Matt as she watched him holding his daughter.

"She's really taken to you. Granted, because of the demands of my work, I haven't been around her as much as I would have liked to, but in all honesty, I've never seen her make such a connection to anyone the way that she has with you," she told Matt.

Her remark had him smiling from ear to ear. "You think so?" he asked, looking down at the bundle in his arms.

"Oh, I know so," Riley assured him. "I might not have seen her as much as I would have wanted to, but I certainly did get a chance to observe her behavior around other people."

He sighed. "I wish I had known about her sooner." There was real regret in his voice.

There was no point in harboring regrets, Riley knew. There was no way to undo that.

"That's all in the past," she told him. "All any of us can do is move forward from here on in. I know that Breena would have wanted you to do that."

The sad smile on Matt's face was philosophical. "You're right," he agreed.

By now, they had reached Riley's vehicle, which was parked off to the side. Riley opened the rear door directly behind the passenger seat.

Matt looked down at the small bundle in his arms, his brow furrowing. "I don't want to wake her up," he told Riley.

"No one said you had to," she pointed out.

Matt was at a loss. He warily eyed the sleeping child. "Then how do I…?"

"Kids are really resilient," she relayed. "Just tuck

Vikki into the car seat. My guess is that she'll probably just go on sleeping."

Matt had a very skeptical look on his face. "You really think so? You don't think that strapping her into the car seat will wake her up?"

"No, I don't," she answered. "And if for some reason she does wake up, she'll probably just fall back asleep." She gave him a slight knowing smile. "It has been known to happen. It's not as if she was an infant you have to tiptoe around."

Matt sighed, shaking his head. "There's just so much to learn."

"The good news," she told him, loosening the car seat straps so that they could be tightened around Vikki once he slipped her into the seat, "is that it is not an impossible task. It just takes a while."

Vikki made a strange noise as the straps were carefully placed around her little shoulders. Matt froze as he looked at his daughter.

"Is she all right?" he asked Riley uncertainly.

He really did have a lot to learn, she mused, feeling sorry for him. But out loud, she went out of her way to reassure him. "She's fine. Kids do make all sort of strange noises, even if there's nothing wrong. Honest," she added.

Matt frowned as he took a step back from the rear door. "You probably think I'm crazy—or at the very least, pretty stupid," he added.

"No to either point. Just inexperienced. No mother or father ever fell from heaven pre-taught," she assured him honestly, quoting an old saying she had once heard. "This whole parenthood thing is one giant learning process." She smiled fondly. "My mother once told me that she was still learning things about being a mother—and at the time she said that, I was convinced that she knew absolutely *everything* there was to know about being a mother."

Moving Matt slightly out of the way, she tested the car seat straps to make sure that they were secure.

They were.

Stepping around to the front of the car, Riley got in behind the steering wheel and buckled up, then waited for Matt to follow suit as he got in on the passenger side.

"So don't be too hard on yourself," she continued. "You didn't know everything when you went into engineering, right? Well, I have it on the best authority that fatherhood is the same thing. And just so you know," she told him, starting up her car, "you'll never know everything. But eventually, you'll get a lot closer to that point than you are right now."

Matt appreciated what she was attempting to do. "Thanks for taking the time to help navigate me through these choppy waters."

Riley inclined her head and responded with a grin as they left the parking area. "My pleasure. Besides, I did have fun today. I always like spending time with Vikki. She's slowly coming to terms with losing her mother and I really enjoy watching her reacting to you," she said with sincerity.

He thought about that and laughed. "I have to admit that I've never been so unsure of myself in my life," he told Riley. "And that's taking my whole dating life into account, as well—not that I ever dated all that much," he qualified. That was why, when he had met Breena, he'd felt as if he had been hit by a ton of bricks. "I have to admit that coming out here to meet Vikki took an awful lot of courage on my part. I had no idea what to expect. That same uncertainty even shadowed me today when we went for our picnic by the lake."

She wondered if he was exaggerating. She supposed it was a possibility. Riley looked at him more closely. "You certainly didn't look nervous," she declared.

"Well, I was," he freely admitted, deliberately keeping his voice low so as not to wake Vikki. "I was worried about making some sort of a mistake. I just didn't want Vikki getting the wrong idea about her father."

"There is no 'wrong idea' to get about her father," Riley refuted. "You showed up, that's the part that counts the most."

Matt smiled his gratitude at her. What she had just said put him greatly at ease. "You know, you're a lot easier to talk to than I'd first thought," he confided.

"I have a tendency to grow on people," she stated with a wink.

Matt laughed softly to himself. "Apparently."

Riley continued to drive toward the ranch house, eager to get Vikki home and put to bed.

Just as Riley had predicted, the little girl was still sound asleep when they arrived.

Matt carefully extracted Vikki out of her car seat. Following behind Riley, he carried his sleeping daughter up to the house.

Mike had apparently been listening for the sound of Riley's car pulling up. He had opened the door and was now holding it for them as the trio entered.

"I was about to send out a search party to look for you guys," he told them, closing the door. Observing the looks on his granddaughter's and Vikki's father's face, he said, "I take it you all had a good time."

Riley grinned. "That we did, Pop," she told him. "Sorry we're late getting back. I'm afraid that time kind of got away from us."

Mike glanced out the window. Everything outside was absolutely pitch black. "It certainly looks that way," he agreed. Then, looking at Matt holding his sleeping daughter, he suggested, "Why don't you help him find his way upstairs—or would you rather that I carried her up to bed?"

"That's okay, we can handle it, Pop," Riley assured him. Looking at Matt, she said, "It's the same room that she's been in."

With that, she turned on her heel and led the way up the stairs.

Matt was right behind her, taking the stairs at a careful pace so as not to jostle the little girl. He didn't want her waking up.

The door to the bedroom he'd read her a bedtime

story in just the night before was open. Riley walked in ahead of Matt and pulled back the covers.

When he set Vikki onto the bed, Riley took off the little girl's shoes and pulled the covers up over her. Matt appeared to be somewhat confused by that. "Shouldn't we, or at least you, change her for bed?" He wanted to know.

"Vikki's really exhausted. I don't want to take a chance on waking her up by undressing her," Riley confessed. "Besides, sleeping in her clothes won't do her any harm." She grinned at him as she stepped back, looking at the sleeping child. "You might have noticed, but I'm not exactly a stickler for rules."

"Yes, I noticed," Matt commented. And then he smiled as he looked at Vikki. "She certainly had fun today, didn't she?"

He saw that the smile Riley flashed at him lit up her eyes. "That she did."

"I had no idea that there was so much joy to be had in having a kid," he couldn't help commenting. "Simple joy," he emphasized.

Riley nodded. He was not about to get any argument from her. "Absolutely. You get to see the whole world through a brand-new set of eyes."

As she stepped outside the room, she closed the door quietly behind her. "Would you like some coffee before I take you back to the hotel?" she queried.

He was not about to ask her for anything. In his opinion, Riley had already done more than enough.

"That's all right, I've taken up enough of your time," Matt told her.

"That's not what I asked you," she pointed out. "Now, would you like some coffee, yes or no?"

"Coffee would be nice," he admitted as they made their way down to the bottom of the stairs.

"The coffee my pop makes is always extremely nice," she assured the man with an amused smile.

"Don't misunderstand…" Matt said, hesitantly qualifying, "but won't it be kind of old by this time of night?"

"It would be," she agreed. "If it was the original pot from this morning, but Pop makes several pots of coffee over the course of the day, so there's always a fresh pot to be had. He *really* likes his coffee," she emphasized.

Riley led the way into the kitchen then gestured toward the coffee maker on the counter. "See? It still has coffee in it."

With that, she took an oversized mug from the cupboard and poured Matt a generous serving. "There you go," she said as she set the mug in front of him on the table. "You take your coffee black, don't you?"

He nodded. "Always." And then he looked around as a thought occurred to him. "Your grandfather was right here. Where did he go?"

"He probably went to bed," she offered. "Now that we've brought Vikki home, he feels that he can rest easy." She saw the bemused expression on Matt's face. "Pop was always like that. If we were supposed to be home at a certain time, he'd stay up until we got in. If we were going to be out for some reason, say over at a friend's house for a sleepover, he made his peace with that." There was a fond smile on her lips as she talked about her grandfather. "For a man his age, my grandfather is very versatile," she told Matt with pride.

"Versatility seems to run in your family," Matt commented.

"I think that's what Breena liked best about us," Riley said affectionately. "She fit right in with us and I'm happy to say that we all really loved her for that."

"And I'm really grateful for that," he confessed. "Grateful that, if I couldn't be around Breena, or there for her, you and your family were."

For not the first time, Riley found herself being drawn to Matt. When she looked up at him, she found herself getting lost in his eyes.

It was a struggle for her to keep the lines drawn.

"You're a very unusual man," Riley couldn't help commenting. "I can see why Breena liked you as much as she did."

"If she liked me…" he began, but then his voice trailed off and he just shrugged. "There's no point in going over that again."

"There's also no point in beating yourself up again," Riley reminded him, her heart going out to the man. "Suffice it to say that there was a great deal of love there and that love went into creating a beautiful child. You can take it from there," she told him. "Okay?"

The stirring within his chest that he was trying to ignore… The stirring that had been there from the moment he had laid eyes on her, and that he had been doing his damnedest to deny, rose to the surface—not for the first time.

Riley saw the expression on his face and couldn't help wondering just what he was thinking. She did her best to repress the question, but it just refused to go away.

She finally gave in and asked, "What are you thinking?"

Matt laughed shortly. "Something that is undoubtedly going to get me slapped."

Riley could feel warmth spreading within her entire body, causing flames to ignite and weave themselves all through her until every part felt as if it was literally on fire.

She folded her hands in front of her and rested them on the table, doing her best to repress the things that she was feeling.

"No slapping," she promised. "Tell me." The request came out in a whisper.

Rather than tell her, he decided to show her, thinking this might be his only chance to do that.

Leaning forward, Matt felt his breath catch in

his throat. The next moment, he tilted his head and brushed his lips lightly against hers.

And then he did it again, but this time with more urgency.

Chapter Sixteen

Riley's heart did not simply speed up. She could feel it slam against her rib cage as it would if she were an Olympic runner urgently dashing to make it across the finish line as quickly as possible. Breathing normally all but became a casualty to that concept.

It didn't matter.

Neither did the wild hammering of her pulse as the kiss deepened.

Until she'd actually kissed him with this amount of feeling, Riley could only pretend that what she'd believed to be true really *was* true. And it was now time to admit to herself what she had always secretly believed. That she cared about Matt.

Really cared about him.

Seeing him through Breena's eyes from the very

beginning, Riley had found herself intrigued by the engineer. But there wasn't anything she could, or would, do about that attraction because, after all, Breena was her best friend and Breena was the one who had fallen for Matt that fateful summer.

But after the summer was over and he had gone back to complete his studies, Riley had been a willing audience to everything that Breena had had to say about him.

When Breena had discovered that she was pregnant, Riley was the one who had urged her to get in touch with Matt with the news that he was about to become a father. After all, from everything she had heard about him, he'd certainly seemed to be loving enough to be a good father.

"Let him know, Breena. He deserves to know. And from everything that you've told me about him, he isn't the kind of person to just leave you flat. I'm sure that he'll want to marry you."

That had been the wrong thing to say to Breena. "I don't want him to marry me because he has to."

"Well then, give him a chance to do it because he wants to," Riley had urged.

But Breena had shaken her head, unwilling to take the chance of enduring a possible rejection, or worse, making Matt feel that he'd had to marry her.

"Please, just let me do it my way," she had told Riley more than once. The discussion had never managed to get past that point.

And there it had remained.

There were times when Riley had been extremely tempted to contact Matt just to tell him that he was about to become a father. But she had honestly been afraid that if she did take that upon herself, she would wind up losing Breena as a friend. She really hadn't wanted to risk that.

So Riley had reluctantly kept her silence and done what she could for Breena and the baby that was to be. In all honesty, she'd been furious with herself for being such a coward and even more furious with Matt for not coming back to Forever in all those years to check on the woman he'd claimed to have loved.

And now he was here, being a father to Vikki rather than fleeing from his responsibility, and Riley found herself falling for him as hard as she had surmised Breena undoubtedly had all those years ago.

Having Matt kiss her the way he was certainly didn't help her to think clearly. As a matter of fact, Riley found that she was having a great deal of trouble thinking at all.

With almost superhuman effort, Riley wedged her hands up against his chest. She managed to create just enough space to allow her to take a breath. Looking up, she saw bewilderment in Matt's eyes. Whether it was because of the kiss they had just shared, or because she had abruptly put a stop to it, she didn't know.

Either way, Riley knew that she needed to get him on his way to the hotel.

Still trying to catch her breath, she said, "I think

I'd better get you back to the hotel before I forget how to drive."

Breathing was a real effort for her, she couldn't help thinking, but somehow she managed.

In all the years since he had been with Breena, Matt realized that he had never reacted like this to what had gone down between them, or even come close to feeling this way. Reflecting on that time, Matt had seriously doubted he would ever have those kinds of feelings again. Those feelings that, echoing all through him, were the kind that, if a person was lucky, they'd experience just once in their lives. In all probability, their very first time, he had thought.

Feeling as if his blood had caught fire was a huge shock. He needed not only to try to calm his breathing, but to clear his head, as well.

"I doubt that you'll forget how to drive," he told her, "but getting back to the hotel right now wouldn't be such a bad idea. It has been a long day."

Gathering her bearings, Riley was surprised she could put one foot in front of the other as they headed for the front door. For a moment, her head felt as if it was spinning, so Riley carefully gripped the banister at the bottom of the stairs and called up to her grandfather. "We're leaving, Pop."

"Wouldn't he be asleep already?" Matt questioned, glancing at his watch.

Riley's mouth curved. "The man sleeps with one ear open," she told him. "He said it's a habit he developed ever since we came to live with him."

"So in other words, ever since you were born," Matt ascertained.

"Pretty much." She led the way out, pausing only to lock the front door. She saw the quizzical look on Matt's face and guessed what he had to be thinking. "Pop likes to leave the front door open. Says it reminds him of friendlier times back in the old days. For the most part, there's nothing to worry about. But in that zero-zero-point-one chance that there might be, my sisters and I feel better about having the front door locked. We tell Pop that we don't want to take a chance on anyone stealing him since he and Mom are the most precious things that can be found in the house."

This time, Matt was the first one to reach the car and get in. That single action reinforced her feelings that he was ready to call it a night.

Maybe he even regretted allowing his feelings to get the better of him. It was a reason for concern, in her opinion. In any case, she intended to have Matt back at his hotel as soon as possible.

As they drove toward town, Matt did his best to try to keep a tight rein on his thoughts, not allowing them to get away from him.

One step at a time, Matt counseled himself. He knew what he would like to happen between himself and Riley, but he was not about to push, not about to presume he knew what she was thinking or feeling.

In all probability, he thought, he could have very well misread the signs, or just been carried away by the moment. The situation he found himself in required careful thought, and exceedingly careful action. After all, he was not the only one involved here. There was Vikki to consider, as well as the memory of Breena.

Maybe his guilt over not returning to Forever until it was too late had caused him to completely misread the signs he'd thought he was getting from Riley.

Hell, no wonder he had avoided getting involved for the most part after he and Breena were no longer together.

Love, or what he presumed to pass for love, was a really very confusing thing, Matt couldn't help thinking.

Neither one of them spoke very much on the way back to the hotel, except to comment on Vikki's amusing behavior during the day at the lake. They both agreed that she was a joy to observe and deal with.

When they finally arrived at the hotel and Riley parked her car in the guest parking lot, Matt came to a decision, sincerely hoping he wouldn't regret it.

It's now or never, he rationalized, forcing himself to push forward.

Turning toward Riley before exiting the vehicle, he asked, "Would you like to come up? Maybe have something to drink? We could talk." He then quickly added as a reminder, "We really haven't had much of a chance to talk yet."

Riley really should turn him down. Saying "no" felt as if it was truly the smart thing to do in this situation. To say "yes" to his suggestion would be like leaving herself wide opened to trouble.

Yet "yes" was the word that rose to her lips.

Or at least some form of it did.

"Sure, why not? We could talk," Riley agreed, emphasizing the word.

They rode the elevator up to his room.

Room service, it turned out, was still available for another hour. "What's your pleasure?" he asked Riley as he picked up the phone to place the order.

She swallowed the incriminating word that first rose to her lips and said, "A sloe gin fizz."

"I haven't heard that one in a long while," he told her before ordering a black Russian for himself. "Are you up for a plate of nachos and a dip?" He wanted to know.

"Sure, why not?" she said gamely. That way, her hands would be occupied, she reasoned.

Room service arrived quickly, bringing the drinks and the bowl of nachos with its accompanying dip within minutes of the order being placed.

The server pushed the small table with the items into the room, had Matt sign the slip, then quietly withdrew.

And then, just like that, Riley and Matt found themselves alone in the room.

Together.

They sat at a small table, slowly consuming what had been ordered. The silence hung heavily between them until Riley finally broke it.

"You know, when you came out here after all this time to finally meet your daughter, I was prepared to hate you," she told him honestly.

"If I had known that I'd had a daughter, I would have been here a lot sooner," he answered. "But I didn't. I didn't know *anything*. Do..'t forget," Matt reminded her, "Breena didn't answer a single one of my calls, my letters or my texts. Nothing. I'm not the kind of person to force myself on a woman, no matter how much I love her."

Riley felt her heart constrict in her chest. Matt was admitting to being in love with Breena. To loving her right from the start.

But then, she thought, she couldn't really think that he had felt anything else. "So you knew you loved her right from the start?" she asked, expecting him to confirm that.

But, in his own way, he wound up surprising her. "I thought I did," he told her. "But—" Matt struggled. "Maybe what I was in love with was the idea of love." He did his best to explain. "Until I had met Breena, I hadn't been involved with a woman to that extent.

"Not to the point that I began to imagine what life would be like with that woman at my side." He sighed as he thought back. "I was utterly crushed that she didn't envision life the same way.

"And then, when I kept trying to contact her, only to be shot down time and again, after a while, I just focused on my career and nothing else."

She wanted to erase the pain she saw in his eyes. "Breena did love you. She never spoke a single word against you. But she knew you had a future planned and she didn't want to be a burden, didn't want to impede that future you saw for yourself. But she did speak very highly of you," Riley affirmed. "So highly, that there were times when I could see myself falling for you." Abruptly, she realized she had said too much. "Or at least hoping to find someone like you."

Matt ignored the drink in his hand as he began to really listen to her, his interest engaged the way he'd never thought it would be again. "And did you?"

This was where she extracted herself from the situation by telling him that she had found someone. That she was engaged or "spoken for."

Or *something*, Riley thought.

But honesty had always been her long suit. So she admitted, "No, I didn't. I have never really been involved with anyone before. My family, my friends, school, and being a nurse practitioner, has always taken up my time," she told him candidly. "All of my time."

Matt set his glass down and moved it aside. "Would you be willing to get involved if someone that you had an affinity with came into the picture?" he asked, watching her lips as he waited for her to give him an answer.

Riley took a deep breath as she shrugged. "I was

taught to never say never." Her voice sounded almost unreal to her own ears.

His eyes never leaving hers, Matt rose from the table, took her hands in his and brought her up to her feet, as well. "By who?" he asked Riley. "Who taught you never to say never?"

"My grandfather," she answered, the words coming as if in slow motion.

"Your grandfather is a very wise man, Riley," Matt told her.

"I always thought so," she whispered, her heart hammering so hard she found it genuinely difficult to breathe again.

Riley was discovering that this was becoming a common condition for her whenever she found herself around Matt.

The next moment, there was no more time for words, no more time to think of anything except the present and the way this man she had technically just met made her feel.

But in all honesty, there was no "just" about it. She had known Matt for what seemed like forever.

And when his lips touched hers, Riley experienced an incredible explosion in her veins that all but dissolved her into a palpitating lump of clay. She melted into his arms, her mouth sealed to his. Incredible as it seemed, something inside her felt as if she had just come home.

Chapter Seventeen

A distant voice in Riley's head whispered that she needed to stop what was happening right now. Stop it while she still could.

But that voice sounded so very distant that she could barely hear it. And right now, she certainly was not in any position to obey it.

Not with her blood rushing through her veins the way that it was. She could feel it demanding that she give in to this desperate hunger that was progressively increasing, growing to greater and greater proportions within her. It had been a long time since she had been with anyone. So long, she couldn't really remember the last time that had taken place.

Or the last time that she had felt this way.

But this was definitely not the time to attempt to

remember anything, except for this incredibly strong desire that was overwhelming her.

And then, suddenly, she felt Matt's lips leaving hers.

He was backing away.

Had he changed his mind? Was he coming to his senses? Riley couldn't help wondering.

Her chest felt as if a jackhammer had suddenly created a hole in her heart. She looked at Matt quizzically. What was happening here? Had he realized that he was making a grave mistake?

Matt was looking at her as if trying to decide something. "Are you all right with this, Riley?" he finally asked, wanting to know.

She wanted to shout, "Yes!" but she knew that she couldn't. The best she could do was ask him for a clarification.

"Define 'all right,'" Riley requested quietly.

Matt took a breath. For a moment, he didn't say anything. And then, "I really want you, really want to be with you," he told Riley with sincerity. "But I don't want to force myself on you, so think about what we are about to do very carefully."

Riley's smile began in her eyes and worked its way to her lips. "Good news," she breathed in a soft voice, "you're not forcing yourself on me."

Still, Matt didn't look convinced. "You're sure?" he asked.

"I'm sure," she answered, her fingers lightly stroking his face. She could see his reaction to her and secretly cheered. "I'll even sign that in blood—later," she told him then elaborated, "Much later."

His eyes held her prisoner for a moment longer. He saw what he needed to in her eyes, then bent his head over her face and resumed kissing Riley with a passion he was no longer afraid to unleash.

Part of him felt somewhat confused at what was happening. Another part of him, the greater part, felt as if he had somehow managed to stumble onto something that was completely brand-new.

Guilt slashed through Matt, telling him he shouldn't be doing this. But within moments—less than even that—that feeling evaporated, burned away by the heat that was being generated.

And then even that wound up disappearing into the mist.

He could feel her heart pounding against his, uniting them. The very thought, the very sensation, excited him to levels he had never experienced before.

Every part of him felt eager and alive.

He didn't remember picking Riley up in his arms. Didn't remember carrying her the short distance to his bed. Somehow, it just happened. And throughout that whole, very short trip, he never removed his lips from hers.

Matt just continued kissing her, over and over again, the fire in his blood growing to huge proportions as his hunger, his desire for that ultimate moment, continued to expand.

Once they were on the bed, their hands flew over

one another, stroking, possessing, and undressing one another while in the midst of a frenzy.

Never in her wildest moments could she have imagined that it would be like this, that the desire to be taken by Matt as well as to take him could pound so urgently through her veins.

Breathing was growing more and more challenging, more difficult for her, but Riley didn't want to slow down, didn't want to stop what she was doing.

Couldn't stop.

She was afraid that if she did, that would suddenly be the end of it. That the multicolored world that had opened up for her would suddenly stop spinning and then just disappear altogether, leaving her saddened, stranded and bereft.

She knew that this was only temporary, that she was only experiencing something she had never felt before because Matt missed Breena with all his heart and was dealing with it in the best way he knew how.

Later, she knew she would have to atone for that, but right now her heart was rejoicing because of the myriad wondrous sensations she was experiencing.

Until this very moment, she realized that whatever else had happened in her life before had only involved going through the motions. Her heart, her pulse, all of it had been dormant until just now. "Now" only served to show her what she had been missing. The sheer joy of lovemaking wrapped itself around her, allowing her to see exactly what hadn't been there before.

She clung to it like a survivor of the *Titanic* to a life raft, savoring only the moment and utterly glad of it. Later, there would be guilt. Later, there would be atonement. Right now, there was just this moment, and that was more than enough.

Matt felt guilt scratching away at him.

He ignored it.

Guilt had no place in lovemaking, especially when his desire for Riley had made him feel as if his very soul had been set on fire.

His lips skimmed along the body that now lay nude next to his, feeding his desire and making that desire grow to higher and higher proportions.

He had given up hope that he was ever going to experience anything remotely close to this feeling ever again. But here it was, making him want the woman he was making love with in ever-increasing magnitudes.

Matt could hardly hold himself in check, grateful for the desire that continued to weave its way through him.

Her breathing was growing more and more pronounced. With her body against his, Riley raised her hips, silently urging him on.

He could feel his heart slamming against his rib cage, desire consuming him, until he finally gave in to the urgency beating through his body and slipped into her, uniting them and making them one.

Finally.

Matt watched her eyes widen as radiance came over her features.

Her arms went around him as he began to move within her, slowly, deliberately, and then with an urgency that completely took her very breath away.

They moved in ever-more-pronounced unison, going faster and faster toward the ultimate soul-satisfying reward they each silently knew was waiting for them.

When it came, exploding within them like wild, sparkling, Fourth of July fireworks, Riley clung to Matt for dear life. Her breathing became progressively ragged until it almost got the better of her.

Slowly, still holding on to one another, they descended to earth, a rosy, warm, satisfying feeling blanketing them both.

It took Riley more than a few seconds to get her bearings.

She almost didn't want to open her eyes because doing that meant releasing her hold on the wondrous sensation that had wrapped itself all around her.

When Riley finally did open her eyes, she found Matt looking down at her. For a long moment, he said nothing. He just lightly stroked her hair and smiled at her.

When he finally did speak, it wasn't what she was expecting.

"Well, that was certainly a surprise," Matt told her.

Confused, she tried to make sense out of his remark. "Why?" She wanted to know, taking offense.

"Because you thought that making love with me would be like making love to a pet rock?"

Stunned by her response, Matt began to laugh so hard that he almost wound up choking.

"No," he said, clearing his throat. "Because I never thought I was going to be able to feel anything even remotely close to what I had experienced years ago with Breena."

Riley knew she wasn't supposed to say anything about what he'd just told her; that in all probability, Matt was just being polite and she should be grateful for his effort.

But she couldn't help herself.

The question seemed to rise to her lips of its own accord, emerging almost like a timid whisper. "But you did?"

"I did," he confirmed with feeling. Taking her hand in his, he brought it to his chest. His heart was pounding hard. "See?"

Her eyes met his as a smile rose to her lips in slow motion.

She knew she shouldn't get carried away, couldn't make too much of the situation. After all, she had limited experience when it came to lovemaking.

"How do I know that doesn't usually happen to you when you make love?" Riley challenged.

"You're a nurse," he pointed out. "You can conduct your own survey to answer your own questions. Meanwhile, you and I can put my theory to the test—that something wonderful is taking place here between us." His smile was slightly hesitant. "Unless, of course, you'd rather not," he said. "That making love with me once was more than enough for you."

Riley looked almost startled at his suggestion. Was that his way of attempting to get out of it? To actually end what was happening between them before it became unmanageable?

"Was it enough for you?" She needed to know.

He kept a very straight face. "We're not talking about me, we're talking about you," Matt noted. And then a full smile slowly rose to his lips. "But, if you must know? No, it wasn't. It definitely wasn't enough for me." Matt gathered his courage to him because it wasn't in his nature to make these sorts of admissions, but he knew that he needed to if he wanted what was happening between them to go somewhere. "As a matter of fact, if we stay in this room, making love with one another until the end of time, it still wouldn't be enough for me."

Her mouth curved. She was beginning to believe him. "I think we'd have to stop to eat before then."

"Haven't you heard of that old saying about living on love?" he gibed, his eyes smiling at her.

"That's only uttered by people who have full stomachs," she pointed out. "Hungry people are far too busy looking for someplace to eat to say that."

"You know, I didn't take you for a cynic," he said with a laugh.

"I didn't take you for someone with a poetic soul,"

Riley countered. She couldn't manage to hold back the grin on her face.

"I guess we both just learned something about one another tonight," he said.

Her eyes were laughing at him, a huge wave of relief washing over her. "I guess so."

His fingers had been lightly skimming along her cheeks, her throat, and now he was working his way down along the body he had just made love to. He could feel his hunger for her growing.

"How do you feel about making love again?" he asked Riley, his voice low and seductive.

"I feel good," she told him, her eyes holding Matt's as she shifted to lie on her back beside him.

Matt nodded, his smile spreading on his lips. "Good," he declared. "So do I."

With that, he leaned forward over her, nipping her lower lip, starting the process of lovemaking, and turning one another on all over again.

Riley's breath caught in her throat as she wrapped her arms around Matt's neck, holding him close to her and kissing him over and over again until they both dissolved into a second wave of incredibly overwhelming heat.

Happiness spread through her like a glowing, ever-growing wildfire.

She gave in to it willingly and, within moments, it consumed her.

Chapter Eighteen

Riley was able to spend two more near perfect days enjoying Matt and Vikki's company. And then she knew that she was going to have to return to life as she knew it.

Bending the rules, she felt that she probably could spend a little more time in their company, adoring them, doing a million and one things together for fun. But Riley wasn't the type to take advantage of a situation, not to mention that she was far too conscientious to stay away from work for that long. No matter what she told herself, she knew that the medical clinic was understaffed, even when they all showed up. Everyone put in long hours at the clinic.

"You'll be all right," she told Matt the evening before she intended to return to work.

He lay in bed with his arm around her, holding her close. "Is that a statement or a question?" Uncertain, he wanted to know.

She thought for a moment.

"A little bit of both," Riley answered. "If nothing else, my going back to work at the clinic will give you a good idea of what life would be like raising Vikki on your own." She took a short breath before adding, "And that in turn will help you decide what your next step will be."

"My next step," he echoed, as if it were a puzzle he was to contemplate.

"Yes, your next step," she repeated. "Whether you take Vikki back to Arizona with you to raise. Or decide to transplant yourself to Forever to raise Vikki here, where she knows everyone." Riley's tone couldn't help but place emphasis on that last part. "Or…?" Her voice trailed off, leaving the question up in the air.

"Or?" Matt pressed, slightly bewildered as to where Riley was going with this.

She turned her body into his. "That's for you to find out," she told him.

He frowned. "To do that, I'd need to have a magic wand."

Riley's lips curved ever so slightly. "Unfortunately, a magic wand is not standard issue with fatherhood—or with motherhood for that matter." She thought a moment, trying to give him a temporary way out for now so that he wouldn't feel as if he had his back against a wall.

"I tell you what, no one is saying that you have to make up your mind right this minute. You can take your time, mull over the situation. You're free to go on with your life as you know it, go back to Arizona. After a bit, you can come here to see your daughter the next opportunity that you get."

In a way, that sounded like the perfect solution. But at the same time, Matt worried about the effect that such course of action would have on his daughter.

"Wouldn't Vikki feel as if she was being deserted?" he asked.

His concern for a little girl he hadn't even known existed a short time ago warmed her heart. Matt was a decent, good man.

Riley smiled at the man beside her. "Vikki is going to be here with my mother, my grandfather, my sisters and, of course, me. Her main problem, if you want to call it that, is going to be finding some alone time."

"Do kids her age really think like that?" He wanted to know.

She couldn't definitively answer him. "Your daughter is a very unusual little girl, so she very well might."

Matt looked at her. Stirrings that were now becoming all too familiar to him were skating madly through his soul. Part of him worried that this might be the last chance they would have to spend alone together, at least for the time being.

"Could we table this discussion for a while?" he asked.

"Sure." A smile slowly rose to her lips. "What do you have in mind?"

Drawing a breath and moving closer to her, Matt raised her chin just a little. And then he brushed his lips against hers.

"This," he answered just before he kissed her with a passion that grew more and more intense with each passing second.

Any further conversation that might have been disappeared, burned away in the heat of the moment.

For all Matt knew, this could very well be the last time he would be experiencing this, at least for now, and he was reluctant to let it go.

He gave himself up to the experience, enjoying Riley and telling himself that, at least for now, tomorrow was a million miles away.

The sound of her ringing cell phone woke her. Reluctantly, she pried her eyes open. It was tomorrow and sunlight was beginning to poke its way into the hotel room.

Riley scrubbed her hand over her face as she smothered a yawn. Sitting up, she couldn't even focus on the phone's screen as she opened it. "Riley."

"Honey, I think you need to come home." It was her mother's voice on the other end of the call.

Riley was instantly awake, her body rigid and at attention as a chill washed over her. It had been years since she had heard anything remotely like the concern she now detected in her mother's voice.

Something was wrong; she could feel it. "What's up, Mom? What's going on?" she asked. Out of the corner of her eye, she could see Matt looking at her, a worried expression on his face. His mind, she surmised, was immediately going to dark places.

"It's Vikki," her mother told her. "She's sick. Very sick," she stressed.

Her mother wasn't the type to panic, but then, Riley reasoned, this was not the standard situation. "Did you take her temperature?"

Matt's body had grown very rigid. There were questions in his eyes, questions that were demanding answers.

"Of course I took her temperature," her mother was saying. "I raised the three of you, didn't I?"

She hadn't meant to insult her mother. "Sorry, no disrespect intended, Mom. What was her temperature when you took it?"

She could almost see her mother press her lips together as she answered, "A hundred and three, ten minutes ago."

Riley fell back on her training. "Start bathing her in cool water," she instructed. "I'll be there as fast as I can. Kids run fevers all the time," she reminded her mother in an attempt to calm her. "You were the one who taught me that."

"I know," Rita answered, her voice very still. "It's still scary while it's happening."

Yes it is, Riley thought. "See you soon, Mom," she said, ending the call and closing her phone.

The moment she did, Matt launched into a barrage of rapid-fire questions. "Vikki has a fever?"

"Yes," Riley answered. She swung her legs out of the bed and got up.

"But she was all right last night," he complained, clearly concerned. "Is your mother sure?"

She knew he was hoping for a different answer, but she couldn't lie to him. "She's sure." He looked so distressed, she had to give him something to cling to. "Kids get sick all the time at the drop of a hat. They also get well just as fast."

That didn't really help, she noted.

Matt was already quickly throwing on his clothes. She noticed that he didn't seem nearly as confident as he usually was. His voice trembled slightly as he asked, "So what do we do?" He wanted to know, in spite of his shaking hands as he put on his shoes.

"I go to the ranch to see just how bad this situation is. You get to say comforting things to Vikki while I make her comfortable. Hopefully, this will already be resolving itself by the time we get there. Some chicken soup, a little orange juice and some baby aspirin, and this fever and whatever else is going on will be gone by tonight." She offered him an encouraging smile.

Matt looked really doubtful about the prognosis

she had just elaborated on. Still, he asked her for re-assurance. "You really think so?"

She was not about to snow him, or to make more out of the situation until she actually knew more. So she qualified her answer to him by saying, "It's highly possible," and then crossed her fingers.

Matt had always been a realist. Life had taught him that. "What if it's not?"

She was also not about to buy trouble ahead of time. "Like the old saying goes, 'we will cross that bridge when we come to it.' It'll do no good to panic until we have all the information in front of us. And then, hopefully, there won't be a need to panic." She stopped getting dressed for a second to look at him. "Vikki needs to have her daddy strong for her. Kids are smart. They pick up on things. You panic, she'll know, and then she'll panic." Her eyes momentarily pinned him. "Have I made myself clear?"

He blew out a breath. "Totally."

She brushed a quick kiss on his lips. "Good. Then let's go," she urged.

They were on the road within less than five minutes.

Matt was still attempting to make sense out of all this. "There are no other kids around for her to play with," he pointed out as they drove to the ranch house. "Where would she have caught this?"

Riley slanted a quick glance in Matt's direction. "Someday, when I have more time, I'll tell you. For now, suffice to say that there are germs everywhere and all you need to do is take in a deep breath." She couldn't help smiling at him. He was almost sweetly innocent. "You really haven't been around kids all that much, have you?"

He laughed dryly. "When would I have gotten the chance?" he wanted to know.

She nodded. "Good point. Welcome to your trial by fire, Mr. Logan," she told him.

When she glanced in his direction again, he struck her as looking rather pale. "Talk to me," she urged. His concern appeared to be eating away at him.

His voice sounded almost shaky as he asked, "Do you think she'll be all right?"

If she hadn't already been in love with him, this would have made her fall for him. "There is no reason in the world to suppose that she wouldn't be. Vikki is a strong, healthy little girl and there are no rumors about the black plague making its rounds in this century," she teased. And then she looked at him in all seriousness. "Matt, you need to lighten up. If Vikki sees you looking at her that way, you are going to wind up scaring her and that, in turn, could very well hinder her recovery. Like I said, kids pick up on things, that includes negative vibes. So think happy thoughts and both of you are going to get through this intact. I promise." As she said the words, she fervently hoped that her positive, upbeat attitude would be enough to convince him.

Matt sighed and blew out a breath, trying to get hold of himself. "You're the doctor," he murmured.

"No, I'm the nurse. A nurse with a lot of experience. Glad we've managed to establish that," she responded with a smile as she stepped down a little harder on the gas pedal.

Riley made great time, although she could see by Matt's expression that it wasn't fast enough for him. When she pulled the car up to the ranch house, Matt didn't wait for her to come to a full stop. She had barely pulled up the handbrake when he all but flew out of the passenger side, dashing up to the door.

Matt remembered to knock, although he knew the front door was unlocked. But even so, after one obligatory knock, he twisted the knob and quickly made his way into the ranch house.

Mike showed no signs of surprise. Instead, he pointed up the stairs toward the bedroom the little girl was currently in. "Rita is with her," he said. "I just came down to get Vikki some water."

"How is she?" Riley asked her grandfather, walking in behind Matt.

"Hot," Mike answered honestly. "But I think she's a little less hot than she was when she first woke up in the middle of the night. At least," he amended with a qualifier, "that's my layman's opinion. I could be wrong."

Riley had her medical bag with her. She kept one in the trunk of her car, another in the house, as well as the bag she resorted to at the clinic. They were all identically packed so she was able to grab any one of them at any moment.

She raced up the stairs ahead of Matt, wanting to get a handle on the situation as quickly as possible.

Vikki looked almost lost in the bed. "How are you doing, little one?" Riley asked her as she walked into the bedroom. She nodded a greeting at her mother.

Her mother, she noted, looked really tired. She had obviously been up all night with the little girl.

Vikki's face was flushed and her eyes looked rather lack-lustered.

"I'm hot, Riley," she complained unhappily. "I don't like being hot."

"Well, we're just going to have to make that go away," Riley promised. Trying to be as upbeat as possible, she wasn't prepared for what Vikki asked her.

"Am I going to die?"

Riley congratulated herself on recovering quickly. "No, of course not, sweetie. Why would you think that?" she asked as she sat down on the edge of the bed.

"Because my mama got sick and then she died, so I thought that would happen to me, too," Vikki explained. Watery eyes swept over Riley and then over her daddy.

Matt was hovering above his daughter, his face looking far more concerned and drawn than Riley had ever seen it. It was obvious to him that the child was very frightened.

"That was a different case, sweetie," Riley assured her. "You're not going to die." She glanced toward Matt. "Nobody here is going to let that happen," Riley promised. "Right?" she asked Matt.

"Right," he agreed, stroking Vikki's damp hair.

A tiny smile of relief appeared on the small, perfect little face.

Chapter Nineteen

"I thought you were going to go to work," Matt said, mentally crossing his fingers that she would remain here.

He was prepared to argue with Riley and use any means possible to talk the woman into staying here so she could take care of his daughter. Doing so might appear selfish, but he didn't care about appearances or labels. All he cared about was having Vikki get well.

Until just now, Matt had had no idea there could be such a difference between a "well" Vikki and one who was ill.

But there was.

A huge difference.

"In case you haven't noticed," Riley told him, "this

is my work. Vikki is sick and I need to do whatever I have to do in order to help her get well."

He looked at her and said, with the utmost sincerity, "Thank you."

Riley shook her head. Matt was missing the point. "No need to thank me. Like I said, treating sick people is my main purpose. Just because the person I'm treating happens to be someone I've known since she was no bigger than a flea isn't the important part. Making sure that she gets well is," she concluded.

Matt looked down at his daughter. She was feverish and seemed almost swallowed up by the bed she was lying in. He hated seeing her like this, hated feeling so helpless.

"What does she have?" He wanted to know.

Riley's heart went out to him. Matt looked way beyond worried, she thought.

"Any one of a number of things," Riley answered. "A cold, the flu, perhaps the beginning of bronchitis—or something else. Only time will tell." She took a few items from her medical bag she could conduct a quick examination and hopefully get some answers so she could begin treating Vikki.

Meanwhile, Matt held Vikki's hand in his. It felt almost hot to him. His concern grew. "Shouldn't we bring her to the doctor? Or just go straight to the hospital?" he asked, thinking that would be the quickest course of action.

"We shouldn't take her to the hospital unless her condition is life-threatening," she told him. "People have been known to go to the hospital with one complaint only to come out with something far worse. And this might make you feel better about the situation—my training qualifies me as the middle ground between a nurse and a doctor." She smiled at him as she continued with her examination of Vikki. "A doctor without all the extra trimmings, if you will."

Matt stared at her as if she had just lapsed into another language. "I don't know what that means," he confessed.

She could go into detail some other time, Riley thought. Right now, she had work to do. "That's okay, I do. Bottom line is that Vikki is in good hands—mine—and if I come up against something I don't understand, I do have medical professionals I can turn to." Riley made a note to herself for future reference about the temperature she had just taken.

Matt had never felt this worried before. It wasn't that he didn't have faith in Riley—he did—but it was just that he had never been up against anything of this magnitude before and it felt as if his daughter's life hung in the balance.

"Make her better, Riley."

In this day and age of people who were intent on watching their backs, people who refused to make promises that might not turn out, Riley snubbed the easy way out, not wanting to snow Matt with a lot of vague rhetoric.

Instead she simply pledged, "I will," as she put her stethoscope and other instruments back into her medical bag. She then placed that bag temporarily out of the way.

Riley turned toward Rita, who had been silently standing off to the side, observing. "Mom, I'm going to need a glass of orange juice, a bowl of chicken soup and some dry toast."

"For you or for her?" Rita asked, nodding at the little girl in the bed.

"For her, Mom," Riley answered. "I need to get some nourishment into her."

That brought Rita to another question she wanted to know the answer to. "Have you two eaten yet?" When neither one of them responded, she had her answer. She nodded her head. "I didn't think so. I'll go down and make up a tray for all three of you." Riley's mother turned and left the room.

Matt felt as if he were floundering and that feeling was becoming more intense. "What can I do?" he asked Riley. He really needed to do something to help out. He wasn't accustomed to feeling so helpless.

"You can sit here and keep her company," Riley advised him, preparing compresses to apply to the still rather warm head and little body. She was concerned that if she didn't manage to get Vikki's temperature under control and down, she might very well be forced to make that hospital run.

Matt looked down at the small face with its closed eyes. His daughter appeared to be fitfully moving around in her bed.

"She looks asleep," he commented. "I don't think she even knows that I'm here."

Riley laughed softly. "Oh, trust me, she knows her daddy's here," she told him, and then assured him, "And your very presence is giving her comfort."

He had his doubts about that, but Riley sounded so convinced, Matt wasn't going to argue with her. "Well then, I guess my path for today is clear," he said as he pulled a chair over to the other side of his daughter's bed and lowered himself onto the seat.

Bending closer to his daughter, he could feel concern well up within him. Matt did what he could to block out that sensation.

"It's going to be all right, Vikki," he promised his daughter, whispering to her. And then he looked up at the woman he was putting all his faith in. "You sure she can hear me?" he asked doubtfully.

"She can hear you." Riley said the words with unshakeable certainty.

Rita and Mike walked into the room shortly thereafter, each carrying a tray with servings of breakfast. There were equal shares for Riley and Matt and a smaller serving of the food that Riley had requested for Vikki.

Matt clearly had his doubts about the meal for Vikki. "She's asleep," he protested. "How are you going to get her to eat?" It seemed illogical to him.

"Have you ever heard of coaxing?" Riley asked, amused.

"Coaxing conscious people, maybe," he allowed. "But she looks asleep."

"She probably is," Rita agreed. "But she can still hear you."

Matt looked at Riley's grandfather for an explanation he could deal with.

Mike merely raised his hands in a sign of surrender. "I learned a long time ago never to argue with a mother. It's a losing battle in more ways than one."

As her grandfather said that, Riley picked up a spoon, dipped it for a tiny drop of chicken soup, and then brought it up to Vikki's lips, holding it there. Very gently, Riley coaxed that spoon between the little girl's lips until Vikki, her eyes still closed, opened them and allowed just a little chicken soup to enter her mouth.

Feeding Vikki was an achingly slow process, but it *was* a process and getting nourishment into the little girl was all that really mattered.

"She's eating," Matt cried, staring at his daughter in wonder.

Riley smiled at him, sharing in his happiness. "Yes, I know," she answered.

Rita looked at Vikki's father. "Why don't you follow suit and do the same?" she suggested. Then, with a wide smile, she told the young man, "You need to keep your strength up, too, Matthew."

In his opinion, Riley's mother was forgetting about someone. "Riley needs to eat more than I do," he returned.

"Don't you worry, young man. Riley will take care of Riley," Rita told him. "She's learned how to utilize her bursts of energy. This, from what I gather, is your first experience with fatherhood. You need to gather up *your* energy." Rita pushed the tray she had brought closer to him, pinning Matt with a look. "Now eat, young man." Riley's mother leveled a pseudo stern look at him. "Don't make me have to tell you again."

Riley looked over toward her mother, the spoon she was using to feed Vikki temporarily suspended in midair. "You could always threaten him with Miss Joan, Mom," she suggested, tongue-in-cheek.

"Threaten me how?" Matt couldn't help asking. After all, the woman was getting on in years and could probably be blown over in a stiff wind.

Mike closed his eyes for a moment as he shook his head, negating the thought. "You really don't want to know."

And then Mike drew himself up. "Well, I've got a ranch to run, but I'll be back soon," he vowed, his eyes sweeping over his granddaughter, his daughter-in-law and the two people who had managed to quickly burrow a place in his heart. "If you need me before then, send one of the ranch hands to come fetch me."

"We'll be fine, Pop. This is not my first rodeo—or my first little patient to nurse back to health," Riley pointed out.

"I know, honey. I didn't mean to imply that you're

out of your depth. I just wanted you to know that I'm here for you if you need me," her grandfather said.

Riley's eyes smiled at the man she had known and loved since forever. "I know that, Pop. I never doubted it for a second. See you later," she told him.

Mike nodded and echoed, "Later," then walked out of the bedroom.

Rita gathered the used dishes onto one tray, leaving the other tray and dishes for later. "Is there anything I can get you or bring you?" she asked, looking at her daughter and Matt.

Riley shook her head. "You've done more than enough already, Mom. If I need you," she assured the older woman, "I'll holler."

Rita nodded, not really completely convinced. "See that you do." She picked up the tray then tossed the words over her shoulder. "I'll be back later."

Matt quickly pushed his chair back and got to his feet. He made his way to the bedroom door and held it open for Riley's mother.

Rita smiled at him. "Nice to know that there are still gentlemen in this world," she said.

"They're there, Mom," Riley said. "You just have to look a little harder for them these days. It's not a badge of pride, the way it used to be."

Rita nodded. "Sad, but true," she agreed as she made her way out the door.

With Riley's mother gone, Matt turned his attention back to his daughter. She had managed to consume close to half a small bowl of chicken soup, all apparently while still asleep.

Matt couldn't get over that. But he turned his attention to a more serious subject. "How is Vikki doing?" he asked Riley, since she was the authority here.

"Well, as you can see, she's still sleeping. But she did manage to get in some soup as well as a little orange juice. That can only help."

But Matt still looked concerned. "Shouldn't she be eating more?" he asked.

"Going a couple of days like this won't hurt her," Riley informed him. "She usually has a very healthy appetite. If she continues like this—not eating much—then we might have a problem on our hands. But not right now." She smiled at him, even though she felt his pain. "Don't buy yourself any trouble if you don't have to," Riley advised. "Vikki is probably going through the worst of it and, in a couple of days, she'll bounce right back."

"'A couple of days'?" Matt echoed, distressed. "She's going to be like this for a couple of days? What if she gets worse?" He wasn't sure he wanted to know.

"Focus on her getting better in a couple of days," Riley stressed.

Matt looked down at his daughter, concern creasing his forehead. "But what if—"

Riley put her finger against his lips, stopping the words he was about to say. "No 'what-if,'" she warned with feeling. "Maybe you'd be better off if you volunteer to help Pop on the ranch," she suggested.

Matt laughed under his breath as he shook his head. "Only if you want one of us to lose a foot or an arm. Right now, I'm much too distracted to handle any machinery—or horses."

"Okay," she told him. "You can stay here—as long as you don't let your imagination run away with you and you don't worry. Just rein in your thoughts and focus on being here for Vikki."

Matt frowned. That did not sound very proactive to him. "Like a lump?"

"No, like a concerned father," Riley corrected. But she could see that Matt wanted to be doing something more than just sitting there, inert.

"You could read to her," she told him. "Or sing," she offered.

"'Sing'?" he repeated as if she had just lapsed into a foreign language.

"You know, music. The thing that poets always said was supposed to soothe the savage breast." Riley's mouth curved as she looked at Vikki's father.

"Are you implying something here?" he asked.

"Nope, not me," she said, crossing her heart to show that she was serious.

Matt suppressed a laugh under his breath. "I think for both our sakes, I shouldn't sing," he told Riley. And then he made a decision. "I'll read to her."

Riley smiled as she nodded at him. "Reading is

good," she pronounced, then went and brought over an oversized book that had been sitting on the bureau.

The book was entitled *Ellie's Big Adventure* and from the looks of it, it was a story about a teddy bear who decided to go wandering one day.

Riley handed the storybook to Matt, thinking that reading this out loud would keep the man occupied. And that, in turn, would be immensely helpful, she added silently.

Chapter Twenty

The small bedroom had gotten crowded after seeing its fair share of activity during the day.

Riley had contacted Dr. Davenport, one of the doctors she worked with at the clinic. She'd given him a quick, educated summary of what she'd felt Vikki had come down with. After ruling out several disease possibilities, she'd arrived at the conclusion that what Vikki had was bronchitis.

Rather than have her bring the little girl in, the doctor had decided to pay Vikki and her family an old-fashioned house call.

"Or," as Riley had told Matt and his daughter when she'd told them about it, "a ranch call."

When Dr. Davenport arrived, she'd noticed that he'd brought several vials of antibiotics with him.

He'd clearly planned to not just inoculate Vikki, but the four adults who were with her. He had even brought a vial for Rosa.

"Can't forget the lady who serves the meals here," Davenport told Riley. Noting the apprehensive look on Rosa's face, the doctor from the clinic told the older woman, "Remember, it's always better to be safe than sorry."

With that, he proceeded to inoculate the entire household.

"Nice catch," he said, congratulating Riley for making the correct diagnosis so early.

Grateful for the compliment, Riley smiled at the physician. "I had a very good teacher," she told him, her eyes meeting his.

The doctor prepared a list of instructions to leave with her, and told her what to be on the lookout for in case the disease took a turn for the worse.

"Although I think we caught it just in time," he told Riley as he prepared to leave the room. "Give me a call later today."

He then paused beside Vikki's bed. "And you, beautiful, just go on dazzling everyone with that smile of yours." Davenport left the little girl with a lollipop.

Everyone thought it was a very good sign that Vikki took off the plastic wrapper and popped the lollipop into her mouth.

"Good to finally meet you," the doctor said to

Matt, shaking the latter's hand. "Although I am very sorry about the circumstances," he added.

"Yeah, me, too," Matt agreed, knowing that the man was referring to Breena's passing.

That had been hours ago. Eventually, everyone had settled in for the night, resting and focusing on Vikki. Although he couldn't exactly pinpoint just when it happened, Matt had finally managed to fall asleep in the chair he had pulled up next to his daughter's bed.

Riley spent most of her time observing Vikki and her father sleeping. The antibiotics had kicked in and put both of them to sleep. The medication, however, had had little effect on her.

Or maybe she just didn't let it because she was so intent on keeping vigil over father and daughter. Whatever the reason, Riley stayed awake for most of the night, watching both Vikki and Matt closely for any signs of a regression.

Her mother came by the room around seven to bring her dinner.

"I didn't bring any for them because I had a feeling they'd be asleep for most of the night," Rita explained. Setting the tray down, she looked at Riley and ordered, "Eat."

Riley waved the tray away. "I'm not really hungry, Mom." Her concern about Vikki, as well as Matt, had worn her out and the first thing to go had been her appetite.

"I didn't ask you if you were hungry," Rita said, pushing the tray in closer to her daughter. "Now eat," she ordered again. Her eyes narrowed slightly as she looked at her daughter. "Or am I going to have to force-feed you?"

She would, too, Riley thought, looking at her mother. "That's all right, Mom. You don't have to do that. I'll eat."

Rita nodded, patting Riley's hand. "Good girl."

Tired, worn out, Riley momentarily struggled not to lose her temper. "Mom, I'm not five years old anymore," she reminded the woman.

Very lightly, Rita ran her fingers along Riley's cheek. "To me, you'll always be five years old, just like your sisters," she told the daughter she thought of as her middle triplet.

She looked pointedly at the dish she was leaving behind. "Now clean your plate, young lady. I'll see you in the morning—unless you need me, in which case, don't hesitate to call," Rita told her daughter just before she quietly left the room and closed the door behind her.

The small bedroom grew incredibly quiet then. Only the sound of even breathing echoed softly around the room. Riley looked at Vikki, relieved that the little girl was on her way to getting better.

"We weathered our first storm, Breena, and we survived. You would have been proud of Matt," she told the memory of her friend. "He turned out to be every bit as loving as you said he was. He certainly came through for Vikki. She still misses you very, very much, but having Matt around like this makes it a little easier for her."

Riley paused, pressing her lips together. "I have a confession to make," she told her friend, continuing to whisper. "I think, listening to you talk about him off and on over the years, you made me fall in love with him. I promise that I won't do anything about it," she said quickly. "But I just wanted you to know," she concluded, addressing the memory of her beloved best friend.

Riley's eyes were focused on the wall and she didn't see Matt's eyelids flutter briefly as he absorbed Riley's words.

"Can we go out and play today?" Vikki asked eagerly. It was morning. Her voice sounded completely different than it had just yesterday.

The little girl, sitting up in her bed, announced in total innocence, "I feel all better now."

The sound of the small voice roused Matt from a rather fitful sleep. His eyes flew open before he was fully conscious.

"Vikki?" he questioned, sitting straighter and looking at the little girl. Every bone in his body was protesting.

"Yes, Daddy?" she asked in completely unaffected innocence, staring at him.

Her color was back. Relief seemed to flood right

through him. "Are you all right?" he asked his daughter in disbelief.

Vikki beamed, her smile wide as it pulled him in. "I'm perfect," she declared. "How about you, Daddy?" She sent him a curious look. "Are *you* okay?"

"Yes," he murmured, hardly aware of the word he had just uttered. Confused, bewildered, Matt turned toward Riley. The latter was silently watching him. He wanted an explanation. "She was so sick, she didn't want to eat yesterday. How could she have bounced back like this just one day later?" He wanted to know.

Riley laughed at his bewildered expression. "Because she's four. Because kids do bounce back incredibly fast—for the most part, they bounce back a lot faster than we adults do," she stressed.

Matt shook his head. In theory, he understood that. But in practice... "These are very confusing waters to navigate through," he told her with a sigh.

"Don't worry," Riley promised, "you'll get the hang of it."

But Matt shook his head. He was far from convinced. "I don't know about that."

"Don't worry, Daddy," Vikki told her father, scrambling up to her knees on her bed. "I'll help you."

She really was a very precious child, Riley thought with a smile.

"See?" she said to Matt. "Problem solved." Out of the corner of her eye, she saw Vikki getting ready to hop out of her bed. "And just where do you think you're going, young lady?"

"To the lake with you," Vikki declared hopefully. "I'm all better," she reminded the grownups.

"And you'll be even better tomorrow," Riley told her with authority. She saw Vikki's face fall. "It won't hurt you to spend an extra day in bed," she added. Looking into the little girl's eyes, she added, "Do it for me and your dad, okay?"

The "okay" that Vikki said sounded far from happy. But Breena had raised her daughter to be a good girl and to be obedient, so Riley was confident that they were on safe ground.

"Maybe," Riley continued, "if you promise to be a good girl, your dad might read you another story or even play a game with you."

Vikki's eyes lit up as she looked at her father hopefully. "Will you?" she asked him eagerly. "Will you play a game with me?"

Matt looked at Vikki. "I'd love to, but I don't know any games," he confessed.

By his count, it had been years since he had played any games at all.

"Everyone knows how to play games," Riley told him. He still eyed her doubtfully. "Lucky for you, we saved all the old games that my sisters and I played." She looked at Vikki. "We played them with your mom," she told the little girl.

That coaxed a smile out of Vikki.

She looked at Riley excitedly. "Can we play one

of those games?" she asked. And then she turned to Matt. "Can we, Daddy? Can we?"

Mentally, he blessed Riley for Vikki's upbeat, eager attitude. Yesterday, he had actually been afraid of losing her. Today, that just seemed like a really bad dream—or more accurately, a nightmare.

Matt felt no end of gratitude toward the woman who had so fortuitously come into his life at just the right moment.

"Do you know where those games are?" he asked, willing to give playing them a try.

"I have total recall," Riley informed Vikki's father. "I know exactly where those games are. Tell you what, I'll bring down a few of them," she offered.

"Can I help?" Vikki asked enthusiastically.

Riley smiled at her. "Not today, sweetheart. Maybe tomorrow," she offered.

With any luck, tomorrow everything would be back to normal, Riley mused. That meant that she would be back to work and then Matt could begin the business of being a hands-on father to Vikki.

From there, Riley thought, they would see where that would lead.

About to leave the room, she nearly walked right into her mother. The latter took a step back. "I've come by to see how the patient is doing," Rita told Riley and Matt, looking at Vikki.

"I'm all better," Vikki announced, beaming. And then she contritely looked at Riley's mother and amended, "Well, mostly."

"Well, that's very good to hear," Rita told the little girl. She bent over and pressed a kiss to the child's forehead. "Yup. Nice and cool," Riley's mother declared.

"Mom, could you stay with Vikki for a few minutes?" Riley requested. "Matt and I are going to bring down some of the old games that Reagan, Roe and I used to play."

"And my mama, too," Vikki piped in cheerily, not wanting them to forget that part.

Riley smiled as she nodded. "And your mama, too."

"Of course," Rita answered her daughter's request. "I would love to spend some time with my favorite short person." Riley's mother took a closer look at the little girl. "You know, you don't look a bit sick to me," she told Vikki playfully. "Are you sure you were sick?" she asked, pretending to examine the little girl a little more thoroughly.

Vikki nodded her head solemnly. "Uh-huh."

"She really likes your mother," Matt commented to Riley as they left the Vikki's bedroom.

Riley nodded. "Uh-huh," she said, imitating Vikki.

"And your grandfather," Matt added.

"Yes, she does," Riley agreed. She stopped at the base of the stairs. She got the feeling that he was trying to say something. "Where is this going, Matt?"

He had been giving things a lot of thought in the

past forty-eight hours. Vikki getting sick this way had completely knocked him for a loop.

"Just that Vikki seems to be really happy here and it might be a problem if I tried to uproot her and take her away," he said slowly.

"Oo-kay," Riley said, drawing out the single word. "So what, exactly, is it that you want to do?"

She waited for Matt to tell her, refusing to speculate on the subject on her own. That might only lead to disappointment.

He, on the other hand, seemed to be waiting for Riley to jump in, but quickly realized she was deliberately waiting for him to speak.

Sighing, he gave in. "Didn't I hear you say that your brother-in-law is an irrigation engineer?"

This was beginning to sound promising, she thought. Still, she struggled to keep the lid down on her hopes. He could very well have something different in mind.

"Yes, he is," she answered.

"I think it might be time for me to meet him," he suggested.

Riley could feel a chorus of church bells going off inside her, heralding the beginning of something that could very well be monumental.

Mentally, she held her breath as she crossed her fingers.

Chapter Twenty-One

Matt looked up the stairs. It wasn't exactly the most private place to conduct this sort of personal conversation, especially since he was putting himself out there.

He knew what he hoped Riley's response was going to be, but he had to admit that he was only guessing. For all he knew, when he put the question to her, Riley might just read him the riot act. Or, at the very least, take offense at what he was proposing.

He had never been so uncertain of anything before in his life. Right now, he felt as if he was walking on a high wire and he was doing it with no net beneath him. So, if he fell, it would be all over for him.

The last thing he wanted was to have someone walking in on them, overhearing what he had to say to Riley. That, Matt thought, would be nothing short of mortifying.

"Would you like to take a walk?" he asked Riley. "We won't be gone long," he promised.

At least, he thought, he didn't think that they would be—unless what he was about to say would wind up triggering a lecture from her. He didn't think it would, but he couldn't really tell for sure.

Going through this wasn't exactly a welcomed proposition, but he knew he had to do it. He had to ask. He certainly wouldn't be able to live with himself if he just walked away. That would be cowardly, and he wasn't a coward.

Riley saw the disconcerted look on his face. She felt a shiver go down her spine.

This could be very good, or very bad, she reasoned. The problem was that she just didn't have any way of knowing which way this was going to go.

She could feel a giant knot forming in her stomach, but there was only one way for her to find out what was on Matt's mind. She needed to hear him out.

Bracing herself—it occurred to her that she was doing a great deal of that lately—Riley took in a deep breath and then said, "Sure. Are we going to be gone awhile?" Unsure just what he had meant by "not long," she was curious. "Because if we are, I'll go and tell—"

Riley didn't get to finish.

"No, we won't be gone hardly any time at all,"

Matt assured her. *Only long enough for you to say "Yes" or "Are you out of your mind?"* The way he saw it, those were the only two options available to her.

Riley gestured toward the front door. "Okay, lead the way," she told him.

Matt did.

He wished now that he had taken the time to rehearse exactly what he was going to say. Practically from the moment that he had arrived in Forever, he had felt himself falling for Riley.

Initially, he had almost thought of her as Breena's stand-in.

But it had quickly become more than that for him.

He couldn't even really explain it to himself. It was just something that had happened naturally, like a flash of lightning.

Almost instantly, Riley had reminded him of Breena. And then, just like that, he'd found himself falling in love with her. He'd tried his best to talk himself out of it, but it was like falling into quicksand. The more he struggled, the deeper he sank.

"What do you want to talk about?" she asked him, feeling extremely uncertain and bracing for anything.

Or so she thought.

But it turned out that she had definitely not braced for what she was about to hear.

Matt took her hand in his and asked, "Will you marry me?"

They had only gone a few feet away from the

house. Riley froze, coming to an abrupt halt. She was positive she couldn't possibly have heard him correctly. He couldn't be asking her to marry him.

Could he?

She stared at him, stunned. "What did you just say?"

He had blown it, Matt thought. But he had never been a man given to flowery words or speeches. He had always said exactly what was on his mind. And, having come this far, he couldn't just walk away from the words that had just come out of his mouth.

He tried to salvage the situation. "It doesn't have to be right now," he assured Riley. "It can be later—a lot later. But I did want you to know what was on my mind—for down the road," he added.

Still very stunned, Riley look at him. "You want to marry me?" she asked, the words all but passing her lips as if in slow motion.

Matt had verbalized what had been on her mind from the very beginning. But now that she'd heard him ask, she couldn't get herself to believe it.

Matt had an extremely serious expression on his face. "Yes."

Riley continued staring at him. She realized that, to believe him, she needed more. "Why?"

He hadn't expected that sort of reaction from Riley. He had expected either a yes or, heaven help him, a no.

"Why do you think?" he said, thinking that what she had just asked him was a very strange question.

"I don't know," Riley answered. "That's why I'm asking you." She spoke ever more slowly. "Why do you want me to marry you?"

For a moment, Matt was at a complete loss for words. And then he pulled his thoughts together and said, "Because this is the only home that Vikki has ever known and she is happy here. Because it's important to me to have her feeling secure. And, most of all, because I realize that I'm in love with you.

"At first I thought it was because you reminded me of Breena. But it's more than that. Being with you makes me happy. I realized that, as much as I loved Breena, I love you differently. And—" he admitted after a beat "—more.

"Now, I'm still going to talk to your brother-in-law and see about joining his engineering firm. I don't mean this to be taken as any sort of pressure from me," he told her. "One way or another, I intend to move to Forever and to make my home here. But that doesn't mean I'm going to try to get you to agree to marry me just because I've uprooted my life and transplanted myself. If you don't want to get married, I can put up with that. Not happily," he admitted, "but I can. As long as you don't wind up shutting Vikki out of your life."

Riley looked at him as if he had lost his mind. "Why would I do that?" She needed to understand.

"To avoid me," he told her honestly.

Riley blinked. The man had spent way too much

time in the sun in Arizona, she thought. Why else would he say things that were half-baked?

"Again, why would I do that?" She wanted to know.

"Because I make you uncomfortable," he said.

Riley cocked her head, as if that might give her a better understanding about what was being said.

It didn't.

"Did I tell you that?" she challenged.

"No," he said helplessly, "but—"

Matt got no further.

Riley pressed her finger against his lips, sealing them. "Then there's no reason for you to believe that."

He stared at her. Hope began to fill his heart.

"Then I haven't scared you off?" he asked.

"No, not yet," she said with a laugh. And then her expression softened. "And there's no reason to believe that you will."

"Then you will marry me? Someday?" he added hesitantly, afraid that he still might scare her off.

In his soul, Matt was convinced that he loved Riley and that he always would, but he knew how that could sound to someone who had been Breena's best friend. For the life of him, he didn't want to do or say anything that would wind up jeopardizing the situation.

Riley realized that she hadn't verbalized an actual answer to his question, even though she felt the answer inside.

"Yes, I will."

"Someday?" he prompted, trying to nail down the answer.

Her smile had filled her eyes. "That all depends on how long you want to wait."

His eyes widened. "Then sooner?" he asked hopefully.

She could feel the smile in her eyes working its way through her entire system. She nodded. "Sooner will be good, yes," she affirmed.

Sooner was too nebulous. He wanted to pin it down further. "When?"

"We can decide that together," she said then added, "After we tell Vikki the good news."

"Sounds wonderful to me," he told Riley.

"But you did forget to say those three magic words," she reminded him.

For a second, Matt didn't understand. And then he asked, "You mean 'I love you'?"

She nodded. "Those are the ones."

Matt laughed at his oversight and shook his head. "You know, being in love with you has been such a part of my thinking from the very beginning that I'd forgotten I hadn't said it."

Matt drew her into his arms. "From now on, I'm never going to forget to say it again—and I'll tell you every opportunity I get, because I do love you," he said just before he kissed her as if his very life depended on it.

Because, in a way, it really did.

Mike Robertson let the curtain drop as he stepped

back from the second-story window. He was smiling to himself.

Two down, one more to go, he thought.

All his girls would be married soon.

For the umpteenth time, he found himself really wishing that Ryan could be here to witness his daughters finding happiness.

* * * * *

SPECIAL EXCERPT FROM

 **HARLEQUIN®** SPECIAL EDITION

*Now that he's going to be rich, bartender Damon
Fortune Maloney can't wait to live his best single
life. So why is the fun-loving bachelor so drawn to
Sari Keeling? The gorgeous, widowed mom of two
is convinced Damon is her Mr. Wrong, but Damon
knows that some rules are meant to be broken...*

Read on for a sneak preview of
Fortune's Fatherhood Dare,
the latest book in
The Fortunes of Texas: Hitting the Jackpot
continuity by Makenna Lee.

Chapter One

The Chatelaine Report: Money must be a great aphrodisiac, as three of the Fortune Maloney brothers have found love since the beginning of the year. There's only one left, but we defy anyone to tie Damon Fortune Maloney down. (Though many would like to!) Everyone's favorite bartender has promised that even after he is wealthy, he has no intention of abandoning the single life. We wonder what it would take to tempt Damon down the aisle...

The day Damon Fortune Maloney left his old, smoking truck on the side of the road and walked into town is the day he used his good credit score and his

name—the one that made people think of money—
and financed a luxury convertible.

With the surround sound playing the latest num-
ber-one country song, he inhaled the rich scent of
leather. The buttery soft upholstery covered bucket
seats equipped with built-in heat, AC and massage
options. The monthly payments were eye-popping
to say the least, but he had a plan. Kind of. His sister
and three older brothers had received their share of
Wendell Fortune's estate a few months apart, and he
was next in line to inherit from a grandfather none
of them had ever known.

Damon pressed the gas pedal and merged
smoothly into highway traffic, the V-8 engine purr-
ing beneath him like a well-satisfied woman. And
satisfaction was something every woman deserved.
It was one of his top rules.

Several heads turned as he pulled into a parking
spot at the Chatelaine Bar and Grill a few minutes
before his shift. There would be questions about his
new car and the assumption that he'd received his
inheritance, which he had not.

It will come soon. It has to.

He couldn't let himself think otherwise. Until
then, he would put off his home renovation projects,
and if necessary, he'd pick up an extra bartending
shift each week. Rather than tossing his sunglasses
on the dash like he'd done with the drugstore pair,
he stored his new designer shades in their case. He
stuffed a few peppermints into the front pocket of

his black jeans and got out of his new silver baby. It locked with a very satisfying chirp of the alarm, something his truck never had. He waved to several regular customers who had paused their conversation to gawk at him. He didn't stop to field questions about his new car. It was Tuesday, and he was never late on ladies' night.

As he neared the front door, a little boy of about six ran over to him with his chocolate Lab on a red leash. He recognized the kid from the T-ball team he'd helped coach. "Hey there, Johnny."

"Mr. Damon, you got candy today?"

"You know it, kiddo." He tossed a peppermint to the child, scratched the dog behind the ears and then waved to the boy's parents, who were whispering as they stared at him.

Turning the heads of most women was something Damon had grown accustomed to, but he didn't usually draw the attention of every man, woman, child *and* dog. The attention was no doubt because of the shiny silver car and his new ostrich-leather cowboy boots. And in the case of the little boy, it was possibly his pocket full of candy. He'd never needed the fancy accessories to get attention from the female population. The car and sunglasses and boots were just whipped topping.

Chatelaine Bar and Grill was painted across one side of the two-story wooden building. The vertical boards were weathered, and the roof was tin, fitting the mining theme of the restaurant. Damon opened the heavy timber door that led into a waiting area with benches. It was decorated with framed photographs and other props paying homage to Chatelaine's mining past.

In the dining room, red leather banquette seating stretched along two walls, some of them tucked into alcoves with mood lighting. There were sturdy wooden tables and chairs in the center and along the back wall of windows that looked out over the patio and the natural area beyond. A couple of firepits, scattered seating and a few outdoor games made the patio a fun hangout place.

Damon clocked in, put on the extra white buttonup from his locker and made his way to the bar that was off to one side near the back of the restaurant. It was a masculine, antique wooden bar that had once been in a saloon.

Like clockwork, the Silver Ladies—a group of elderly women who had a walking club—arrived with their usual enthusiasm. After a bit of harmless flirtation, they would order their usual one glass of wine and salads before going home to watch their "shows."

"Hello, lovely ladies. How are all of you this evening?"

"It's Silver Ladies," the petite one with lots of jewelry said, and smoothed her gray hair as if to point out the reason for the name.

"My mistake. You should add lovely to the name," he said, mirroring her smile.

"Look at you, young charmer, making Marybelle

titter like a schoolgirl," said the tallest of the group, but she looked equally thrilled by his suggestion.

He loved making them smile and giggle. In his book, no woman was ever too old for flattery. After filling their drink order, he poured beers for Alec Ramsey and Paul Scott, who had picked out a center table to wait for the rest of the GreatStore employees who were meeting up tonight. Damon had never worked at the one-stop-shop store where you could buy everything from groceries to new tires, but a good portion of the town's younger residents had worked there at one time or another.

Damon waved to his brothers Lincoln and Cooper as they neared the bar. So much had changed for them lately. Linc was the oldest and most serious of the four brothers, and it wasn't all that surprising that he was engaged to Remi, a wonderful woman who seemed to be just what his brother needed. But shockingly, Cooper, the wild child of the family, was engaged, and Alana was expecting a baby.

All three of his brothers had settled down, but Damon was definitely not following them down that path. At least not yet. He had big plans to live up the single life, especially once he was a wealthy man.

"Where are your better halves?" he asked, referring to Remi and Alana.

"They'll be here in a minute," Linc said. "I'll have the usual, and Remi wants red wine."

Cooper shifted his cowboy hat. "Alana wants a

sparkling water with mint and lemon. She's been having some interesting pregnancy cravings."

"I can do that. Is Max coming Tonight?" Damon asked about their other brother.

"No," Linc said. "Eliza has a real estate event they had to attend."

Damon grabbed a mug, filled it with the Rising Fortune's IPA on tap and then handed it to Linc. He stuck a second mug under the Shiner Bock tap just as Remi and Alana came inside, and they weren't alone. The strikingly gorgeous woman between them was no one he'd ever seen. He would've remembered this goddess with her long, wavy red hair and crystal blue eyes he could happily get lost in. His surroundings blurred, except for the music, and he wasn't entirely sure if it was playing on the sound system or in his head.

Damon jolted when foamy beer overflowed the mug. A cold wet hand and his brothers' snorts of laughter jerked him the rest of the way out of his fantasy. *Well, hell.* He yanked the bar towel from his waistband.

"Head in the game, bartender," Coop said. "I'm not paying for that beer you're spilling."

Linc took a sip of his perfectly poured IPA. "Coop, you could buy the whole keg and not even notice."

Damon ignored his siblings and stole a few more glances at the beauty while cleaning up spilled beer.

"Speaking of buying things… Setting up a room for the baby is majorly expensive. Do you have any idea how much stuff one baby needs?" Coop asked, as if their oldest brother hadn't pointed out the fact that he was now a millionaire.

"No idea." Damon set a fresh mug of beer in front of Coop and started on drinks for the women. Obviously, his brothers had not heard about his new car, because if they had, he would've gotten the third degree straight away. But in this small town, it was only a matter of time before everyone knew. His defense? It was hard watching his three older brothers and his sister living in comfort and wealth while he still had to scrimp and scrape to make ends meet after paying the mortgage on his 1970s fixer-upper. This wasn't the place where he wanted to get into the fact that he'd spent money he didn't have yet.

"Who is the woman sitting between Remi and Alana?" he asked.

Coop chuckled. "So, that's who you were gawking at. That's Sari Keeling. She works with Alana at GreatStore, and they have become friends."

As if Sari had heard them talking about her, she looked straight at Damon. Her lips parted slightly, and her eyes widened before she quickly ducked her head. He could take her reaction in a couple of ways. One, she was shy. Two, she didn't return his interest. Her eyes flickered his way once again, briefly, but he'd caught it. He decided to go with the shy version and see where it took them.

"Sari seems nice," Linc said, and grabbed Remi's wine. "You should come over and say hello to her."

His brothers took their drinks and headed back to the table of friends. Damon liked his job, but missing out on happy hour with friends was a drawback. He served more beer, a few mixed drinks and a scotch on the rocks, then looked around and saw that everyone had a drink, except for the woman he needed to meet. A minute later, Sari headed his way.

Some of her auburn hair fell over one shoulder, trailing almost down to her waist. He imagined what it would be like to run his fingers through the wavy strands and heat washed over him. "Welcome to the Chatelaine, Sari. I'm Damon."

Her head cocked to the side. "How do you know my name?"

"Special bartender powers."

She glanced over her shoulder to the table of friends before turning back to him with a smile. "I guess you know everyone over there?"

"I do. Linc and Coop are my brothers. What can I get for you?" He definitely wouldn't mind getting Sari's phone number and a date. And once he was wealthy like his siblings, he'd love to wine and dine and spoil this woman in style.

Sari spread her hands on the dark wood bar top as if it were grounding her. Her fingers were long and elegant with no rings and cotton-candy-pink polish on her nails. How would they feel scraping lightly over the skin on his back? He shivered at the idea of it.

"I guess…" She drummed her fingers while looking at the bottles lined up behind him on the shelves. "A white wine."

"You don't sound very convinced." He chuckled and leaned his forearms on the bar top, putting them a few inches closer together. Close enough to catch the scent of peaches. "I can mix a special cocktail just for you. Do you like strawberries or raspberries?"

"Raspberries. They are sweet but also tart on your tongue."

Just hearing her talk about something being on her tongue made his mouth water. "Good choice. Are you okay with rum?"

"Yes, but no tequila." She shuddered and got that look on her face that told him she'd once overindulged on that particular liquor.

"Got it. Do you trust me?"

She studied him while worrying her bottom lip with her teeth. "Hmm. I'm not usually much of a gambler, but since it's a rare night out for me, I'll go for it."

"If you don't like the drink, I'll make something else or pour you that glass of white wine, because I never let a woman leave unsatisfied."

Sari pressed her lips together and her eyes scanned what she could see of him. "Is that so?"

"It's one of my top rules."

"What are your other rules?" she asked, and took a seat on one of the barstools.

He was happy to see she wasn't in a rush to get away from him. "Oh, I can't tell you yet. I have to really know someone before I reveal all of them." She was coming out of the shyness he'd first sensed, and he liked it. He dropped fresh raspberries and a couple of lime wedges into a shaker.

With her elbows on the bar, she propped her chin on her clasped hands, watching him intently as if she'd be expected to make the next drink. "We've only just met, and I already know two of them. You like to satisfy women, and you don't share all of your rules at once."

"It must be a sign." Damon added sugar to the fruit and muddled them together.

"A sign of what?"

"For one, that you are very observant, and that we should spend some time together so you can discover the rest."

"What do you call this drink?"

"I haven't decided. It's like a raspberry version of a mojito. Maybe you can help me name it after you taste it."

"Maybe I will."

He added a few mint leaves and white rum, gave the mixture a shake, and then topped it off with sparkling water. "Have you been in here before?"

"It's my first time."

"Firsts can be the start of something good." What firsts could they discover together?

"Only good?" she asked in an innocent voice, but her eyes sparked with playfulness.

I think I could love this woman.

"Possibly mind-blowing." He stuck a bright yellow straw in her drink. "Time for the test. And it's on the house since you will help me name it."

With her pretty pink glossy lips wrapped around the straw, she sipped and made a satisfied sound. "Mmm. It's delicious."

A customer stepped up to the bar before he could figure out a way to tell her he'd like the opportunity to show her how delicious they could be together. "Don't go anywhere. I'll be right back."

What rotten timing to have the other bartender running late and one waitress out sick. While mixing a margarita, he watched Alana give Sari a thumbs-up and then they did some kind of coded hand signs that he couldn't make sense off, but they seemed to be entertained by their silent conversation. To his delight, Sari did wait while he served several customers. Once he got back to her, half of her drink was gone.

"So, have you thought of a good name?"

She licked her lips. "I'm thinking... Berry Delish."

"Hey, Damon. Can I have a set of darts?" a young man asked.

"Sure thing. Just bring them back when you're done." He reached under the bar and grabbed the red and blue set.

Sari turned to see where the guy went. "There are dartboards here?"

"Three of them. You play?"

"I haven't in a while, but I used to be pretty good."

When he played, he almost always won. "I have a break in a while. Want to play a game?"

"That sounds fun, but right now, I should stop monopolizing your time." She stood and picked up her cocktail. "Let me know when you go on your break."

"You got it."

While he worked, Damon was having a hell of a time concentrating and made a couple of drinks wrong, but sharing several smiles with Sari made it worth the extra work. When the second bartender finally arrived, Damon told him he was taking a longer break than usual.

He motioned to Sari in a way that asked if she wanted a second drink, and she nodded. He mixed it, grabbed the darts and was glad when Sari got up to come over to him. If he went over to the table, that would waste too much time talking to the group, and he wanted to spend every minute of his break getting to know her.

"Thank you," she said as she drew close and took the glass from him.

Damon stopped in front of the dartboards that were tucked around a corner, so there was no chance of stray darts accidentally flying toward customers having dinner. "You work at GreatStore?"

"Yes. Since February."

"Where did you live and work before that?"

"In San Antonio. I worked at a grocery store and then a pet store. I get around," she said with a smile.

He set the darts on a tall pub table. "Do you get bored easily and need a change?"

"No. I need flexible hours, and employers aren't always flexible. So I've had to change jobs more frequently than I'd like."

"You should bartend here with me. I'd love to train you." A pretty pink flush bloomed on her cheeks and her soft laugh made his skin tingle.

"I'm not a night owl, and I'll probably be ready to go home by eight o'clock."

Damon looked at his watch. "That's a real shame. All the best stuff happens after dark."

"Not in my house." She hitched both of her thumbs toward her own chest. "Single mom with two toddlers. Ages two and four."

Damon's eyebrows arched at two different angles. "Really? I almost carded you because you barely look old enough to drink."

"I'm definitely old enough for a lot of things."

He liked the sound of that and wouldn't mind exploring the topic a bit more. "I'm twenty-seven, and you must be younger than me."

Sari smiled while sipping her drink. "Thanks for the compliment, but I'm old enough that I could have been your…babysitter. I'm thirty-two."

"No way." He would have loved having her for a babysitter. He had appreciated the beauty of women for as long as he could remember. Neither her age nor the fact that she had children was a deterrent. "I'm great with kids."

"Oh, really?"

"Probably because I'm a big kid myself. I've never met a kid I couldn't babysit."

With her head tilted, she studied him for a moment. "I dare you to babysit my kids."

Chapter Two

Sari Keeling couldn't believe she was flirting with the guy who had caught her attention at the Valentine's Bachelor Auction. The really handsome one she had thought about more than once over the weeks since then. Up close, Damon was even more appealing and gave off a sexy vibe that made her tingle with sensations she hadn't felt in quite some time. He hadn't seemed shocked at her dare to babysit, but no doubt his senses would kick in at any moment.

Damon held up a purple dart. "Want to make a friendly wager?"

Or he'll just change the subject. "What do you have in mind? Something other than money?"

"If I win the game of darts, you agree to go out to dinner with me one night soon." He rolled the dart between the pads of his thumb and pointer finger. "And if you win…you get a free night of babysitting."

Surprise, surprise. Maybe he's braver than I thought.

"Deal." She held out her hand, and when they shook, a tingle spiraled through her body, followed by a shiver that she knew he'd felt, too.

His white dress shirt was unbuttoned just enough to reveal a black T-shirt beneath, hinting at the bad boy she thought he might be. One she probably should not be getting mixed up with. Damon wouldn't know what to do with someone like her. Her life came with a list of responsibilities and challenges that would likely make his head explode.

"Want to be the green or purple darts?" Damon asked.

"Purple, please. It's my two-year-old's favorite color."

"You throw first," Damon said, and put three darts on her open palm.

The brush of his fingers against her skin made her want to shiver again, but she tensed her muscles. "Get ready to lose."

"Trash talk. I like it."

She got into the throwing stance her cousin had taught her, wiggled her hips into the correct position and let the dart fly. It landed just right of the bull's-eye.

"Not bad," he said. "Do you have boys or girls or one of each?"

"Two boys." She glanced at him over her shoulder. "Are you trying to distract me?"

"Never." His crooked grin told an entirely different story.

What would've happened if she had bid on him at the bachelor auction and they'd gone out on a real date? She remembered reading in the auction program what he'd offered. A sunset dinner cruise on Lake Chatelaine. An evening that sounded very romantic. She almost laughed aloud when she remembered the woman who had won him was in the range of eighty to ninety years old. His smile had never faltered as he'd taken her by the arm and guided her back to her table. This bad boy seemed to have a lot of heart.

There could never be anything serious between her and Damon. He was too young and unencumbered and wouldn't understand her level of responsibility, but he sure was fun to hang out with. And to think she almost hadn't come out tonight. But when her neighbor, Mrs. Mata, offered to watch the boys for the evening, she hadn't been able to resist.

Sari threw another dart, landing on the other side of the bull's-eye. She wasn't doing too bad for not playing in forever.

"Where are your kids tonight? With their dad?"

A flash of pain threatened to derail her good mood, but she'd become good at hiding it. "No. My next-door neighbor is watching them. This is a rare night out for me." So she intended to enjoy her time while she could.

"Young ladies like you should get out more than rarely."

"You think so?" Proof he didn't understand a single mother's world, and their flirting could not be taken seriously. It was flattering that Damon thought she was so young, but she felt years older than thirty-two. Life had delivered a series of curveballs and seen to aging her emotionally beyond her years, and she'd bet she had life experiences and challenges he had not. Damon was around the same age her husband had been when they'd married. But she and Seth had been at the same stage of life with plans to take each step and meet every challenge together.

She knew better than anyone…plans could change in a heartbeat.

A familiar but unwelcome heaviness tried to settle in her limbs, but she resisted the pull. She and Seth had had a beautiful life together, until it ended five years after their wedding. But she didn't want to share any of the details with Damon. It always brought down the mood, and she really didn't need any more pitying glances.

She threw her third dart and it hit home, square in the center. She heard his surprised oath before she turned with her arms raised high and did a celebratory shimmy dance, then retrieved her darts. "Your turn."

"I better be on my game tonight." He grabbed his

darts, his arm brushing hers as he moved by, leaving the scent of leather and spices to tickle her nose.

Damon did well but not as well as she had. They were neck and neck, their points shifting back and forth between them, much like their flirty banter.

When she threw her final dart, it was a dead-on bull's-eye, making her the winner. She gave a little hop and cheer, then turned to see the shocked expression on his handsome face.

"I can't believe it," he said, and rested both arms on the tall pub table. "I haven't lost at darts in a long time. And you only said you were 'pretty good.' Was that luck, or are you an undercover professional dart player?"

She took a sip of her delicious fruity cocktail. "I'm no pro. And don't worry about the bet. I won't hold you to babysitting. The look of surprise on your face was more than enough satisfaction." She reached across the small round tabletop to pat his forearm. Damon covered her hand with his, and warmth radiated up her arm. She told herself to pull away, but she couldn't make herself break the contact. It was a connection she'd been craving and not even known it.

"And if I remember correctly, you did say something about women and satisfaction."

He chuckled. "I did say that, and I meant it. And I won't back out of our bet."

She forced herself to slide her hand out from under his and bit the inside of her cheek, suddenly unsure about the bet she'd made without giving it any real thought. Two drinks had gone to her head, and it was a good thing she wasn't driving tonight. "Now that I think about this wager, I don't know if babysitting is a good idea."

"How hard can it be to watch two little boys? I grew up with three brothers and a younger sister. You can't scare me."

Sari paused and looked him up and down from his head of dark brown wavy hair and moody brown eyes, along his lean muscular body to his fancy cowboy boots. "You haven't met *my* kids. They might tie you up with jump ropes and make you watch the same episode of *PAW Patrol* over and over. And over," she said in an exaggerated tone.

"I've never met a kid I couldn't win over," he said confidently.

Or a woman, I'd bet.

Sari suddenly snapped into the reality of her life with a prickle of goose bumps. What was she thinking? She couldn't let a guy she'd just met babysit her boys. Benjy and Jacob were her life. Her everything.

Damon shifted a bit closer. "I can see the worry on your face, and I understand your concern. You don't really know me." He flashed another of his gorgeous lopsided grins. "Yet."

Something tingled deep inside her. Did he truly want to get to know her?

"You should get references," he suggested.

Glad that he understood her concern, she relaxed

just a bit and picked up her drink. "And they will no doubt tell me that you are a fantastic guy?"

"Let's find out." He took hold of her free hand and led her over to the table of friends.

The warmth of his hand felt good. She should be surprised or uncomfortable about the contact, but she wasn't. How could it feel this natural to already be holding his hand?

"I have an announcement." He raised their joined hands, presenting her as champion after one game of darts. "Sari has beaten me at darts."

Some of them laughed and others cheered for her. She liked that he wasn't too cocky to admit he'd been beaten. Damon was fun and easygoing and had a magnetism that drew her in. She liked him way more than was smart, but how was she supposed to control this burst of attraction sparkling between them?

He lowered their hands, but he did not let go. "And now, I need references before I can pay my debt and babysit her kids. Who's got something good to say?" Damon asked the group.

"Well…" His brother Cooper feigned difficulty thinking of anything nice. "He's not a criminal."

Damon groaned. "I should have known y'all wouldn't be any help."

"He can watch my kids," Linc said.

His fiancée, Remi, shook her head. "You don't have any kids."

Linc just grinned and kissed her.

"I plan on letting him watch our baby," Alana said and spread both hands on her pregnant belly.

Sari turned her face to Damon. "Does it scare you to think about taking care of a baby?"

"Nope. As long as I'm not expected to wear that trippy male breastfeeding contraption we saw in that video." Damon gave a little squeeze before letting go of her hand. "I have to get back behind the bar. Everyone behave so I don't have to toss you out."

Sari was so tempted to watch him walk toward the bar but forced herself to focus on the people at the table as she took her seat between Remi and Alana.

Remi ran her fingers through her dark hair. "Girl, it didn't take you but a second to catch the eye of one of the hottest bachelors in town."

"Hey," Linc said to his fiancée. "Don't be saying my brother is hot right in front of me."

Remi rolled her eyes. "I meant like in high demand."

Linc's eyes narrowed as he rubbed his jawline. "I *guess* that's true."

"But he is hot," Remi said in a fake whisper that made Linc grimace.

Sari had worried about being a stranger in her new small town and having no friends in Chatelaine, but she really liked this group and was glad they'd talked her into coming out with them tonight.

When it came time for Alana to drive her home, Sari went up to the bar to say good-night to Damon. "Thanks again for the drinks and the game."

"You bet. I enjoyed our time together. Since I usually work nights, how about I babysit on a Saturday during the daytime? You can have a girls' day out or something." He pulled his cell phone from his back pocket, opened his contacts and handed it to her. "I need your number so we can finalize our plans."

"Did you lose the bet just to get my number?" she asked while typing it in.

"Pretty slick way to get it, right?"

She laughed and handed his phone back. "If you say so."

He touched his phone's screen and hers rang in her purse. "And now you have my number. I'll call you to set up details about babysitting."

"That works. Have a good night." Sari waved, and when she turned to go, a man stepped into her path.

"I'm gonna buy you a drink." He swayed unsteadily into her personal space.

She wrinkled her nose against the reek of alcohol, garlic and sweat. An unpleasant feeling snaked along her spine. "No thank you." When the man stumbled forward again and reached out to touch her, she stepped back even more, bumping into a barstool.

Damon was suddenly between them, and she hadn't even seen him come out from behind the bar. "Time to go home, Bud. I'll call you a cab."

The man swayed to the side. "Don't need a cab. My brother drove."

Damon made eye contact with another man who was walking toward them.

"Sorry. I'll get him out of here." He put an arm around his inebriated brother's shoulders and steered him away.

Damon reached forward as if to touch her but instead put his hand in his pocket as though reminding himself that touching her right after stopping a groping drunk guy from doing the same was not a wise decision. "Are you okay, Sari?"

"I'm fine. I've handled worse than him, but thanks for the assistance."

"I didn't serve him enough to be that drunk. Guess he came in already halfway there."

Alana called her name from the table and said they'd be outside.

"I better go," Sari said. "See you soon."

"You bet you will. Good night." He moved to go but paused and turned back. "Let me walk you to the door, just in case anyone else is misbehaving."

She started to argue that she was not the one who needed a babysitter, but in her book, chivalry should never be discouraged. And it felt kind of nice to once in a while be looked after. "Thank you."

He placed a hand lightly on her upper back to steer her through the dining room to the front door and out onto the sidewalk. "Good night, Sari."

She took a few steps backward to let him—and herself—know that even though it was tempting as hell, any more physical contact would only tempt her to lean in for a kiss. "Good night." She smiled once more, then turned for the car.

"You won't have to fight off guys like him if I'm around."

She wasn't sure if he'd meant for her to hear his statement or not. Was he trying to be her knight in shining armor? Was he really that kind of guy? She always told people she didn't need a protector, and she didn't.

But it might be nice to once in a while have someone to watch her back.

Sitting behind Cooper in the back seat of Alana's car, Sari's thoughts kept drifting back to Damon and the way he laughed easily. The way his quick smile reached his eyes. And the way he had sensed her uncertainty about babysitting her precious boys. If she was going to see him again—and that was highly likely since Chatelaine was a small town—she had to decide now what she was willing to let happen between them. Even after only the small amount of time they'd spent together, she knew remaining strictly friends with a man like Damon was going to be a tall order. Just like he was. Tall and very nicely sculpted, but not too bulky like he spent every day in the gym.

She would make it clear that she was not looking for a romance or a relationship. Not being on the same page had the potential to make things very awkward, and Sari hated it when things became awkward. It made her uncomfortable, made her want to stay in her house and avoid the situation. Being a busy single mom, she did not have the luxury of staying home whenever she wanted.

Keeping Damon in the friends-who-flirt zone was the safest, smartest option, but not nearly as appealing as one that involved touching him in ways friends normally did not. It had to be the alcohol that was making her act like she was in high school, because it wasn't like her to have such an instant crush. Was Damon the best option to be the first person she dated since Seth?

In the front seat, Alana and Cooper were discussing some of the houses and properties they were considering buying.

In a tender gesture, Cooper reached across the space between them and brushed his fingers through Alana's long blonde hair. "I think we should go with the ranch that has the little guest house. It's the perfect size to turn into your photography studio.".

"I really do like that one," Alana said.

Sari leaned toward them. "That sounds like the perfect thing for you. You know the boys and I will be your first customers. And speaking of my boys, is Damon really responsible enough to take care of my kids for a few hours?"

Cooper chuckled and then shifted in the front passenger seat so he could see her in the back. "He's my little brother and I tease him, but he is responsible and won't let anything happen to your kids. He's good with our sister's son."

"You don't need to worry." Alana put on the

blinker before turning into the parking lot of Sari's small apartment complex. "Coop is right."

That made Sari feel a little better about the whole babysitting thing.

Alana put the car in Park and turned to look at Sari. "My baby bump is to the point where I'm having trouble getting to my feet, and I need a pedicure. Want to go do that with me on Saturday? My treat."

"I haven't had a pedicure for ages. And since I suddenly find myself with a babysitter, that sounds perfect."

"Oh, good. Call me tomorrow and we can figure out a time," Alana said.

Sari opened the car door. "I will. Thanks for the ride."

She waved as they drove away, then walked across the center courtyard of her small U-shaped apartment complex of twelve units. As she unlocked her door, she could hear the TV softly playing.

Mrs. Mata, a former elementary school teacher, turned off her movie. "Did you have fun tonight?"

"I did. How'd the boys behave for you?"

"We did just fine." She got up from Sari's overstuffed red chair, her silver-streaked black hair falling in a sleek bob to her shoulders. "Only one episode of their cartoon and a mild fight over the last granola bar, but we got it worked out quickly by splitting it in two."

"I really appreciate you watching them tonight."

"I'm happy to help. I know what it's like to be a

single mom." Mrs. Mata picked up her keys from the coffee table. "Playing with them helps keep me young."

"Well, I'm happy to share them anytime you want." Once Sari had locked the door behind her neighbor, she went down the hallway to look in on her boys. They were sound asleep. With a thumb in his mouth, Jacob was on his tummy with his knees tucked up under him and his little bottom in the air. Benjy was sprawled out like a starfish with his feet on the pillow. She tiptoed closer, and in a well-practiced move, she turned her oldest around, smiling when he mumbled in his sleep. She lightly kissed each of them and then watched them sleep for several minutes.

Her love for them swelled inside her. These boys were her life. The best of her and Seth combined to create these wonderful little humans, and she would do anything to protect them. She saw little bits of Seth in the way Benjy smiled with one eyebrow lifted, and the way Jacob's hair swirled in two directions at the crown of his head. Even after two years, she still couldn't believe her husband and father of her children was really gone. And in such a shocking way. Without a moment's warning, she had joined a club of women who were working every day to hold a family together all on their own.

Even when I'm exhausted.

If things with Damon went beyond his day of babysitting, she'd make it clear she was not looking for a boyfriend. The last thing she needed was another male to take care of.

She slipped quietly from their bedroom and undressed before grabbing her pajamas. A hot shower relaxed her, and she couldn't wait to fall into her bed.

"Mama," Jacob called from across the hallway.

She sighed and turned off the bathroom light, heading for their room rather than her own.

Chapter Three

The out-of-tune melody of Damon's doorbell woke him way before he wanted to open his eyes. Just one more thing in his outdated house that needed replacing. When he convinced himself that the sound was part of a dream and rolled over, someone started knocking on his front door.

"This better be something good."

He climbed out of bed with a groan, pulled on a pair of athletic shorts and made his way through the dining room to the front door. Glancing through the peephole, he saw his brother Linc. He groaned even louder because he had a feeling he knew exactly what this early-morning visit was about.

With a frustrated twist, he unlocked and opened

the door. "Why are you here so early? You know I worked late."

Linc hitched a thumb toward the shiny new car in the driveway. "What's that?"

"It's a car that won't break down on the side of the road." Damon had known this was coming, but did it really have to be this early in the morning and before his coffee? He left the door open and turned for the kitchen, knowing his brother would follow.

"Did you get your inheritance check and not tell any of us?"

"Nope." He pushed Start on the coffee maker. "How did you find out about my new car?"

"I was driving by and saw it." Linc sat in one of the creaky chairs around the hand-me-down kitchen table.

Damon really wished he'd already fixed his garage door, so he could've parked his new car out of view.

"At first, I thought it might be a woman who stayed over, but your truck wasn't here. And the way you looked at Sari last night, I didn't think you'd brought someone else home."

His brother had that part right. Sari was the only woman on his mind. The only one he had a desire to bring home.

"This isn't how Mom raised us. What do you think she'll say?" Linc asked him.

"I'm sure she'll have plenty of opinions to give, as usual."

"You could always sell your house and move in with Mom," Linc said, unable to keep a straight face.

"Shut it, dude. Not funny." Their mom had done the best she could raising five children alone, but having a husband walk out the door when you were pregnant with your fifth child would make anyone rigid about routines and a little bitter. He barely remembered their father, Rick Maloney, who had also grown up without a dad around.

"You can't be spending money you don't have. What if for some reason your check never comes?"

A cold wave slapped him, and Damon glared at his oldest and bossiest brother. He hadn't even considered that possibility. "Why in the hell would you say that? Do you know something I don't?"

"No. I'm just making a point. You need to be patient, little brother. Buying big things on credit is not how we were raised."

The rush of panic eased, but a new whisper of "what if" hovered in his head. "You already said that. And it's easy for you to say that *now*. You aren't having to live like we used to. None of y'all are." He poured a cup of coffee and motioned for Linc to grab a mug. "Do you know what it's like watching all of you live it up and be able to buy things for Mom while I have to scrimp and save to make ends meet?"

Linc poured coffee into a Chatelaine Fire Department mug, added a spoonful of sugar and seemed to be truly considering this concept.

Damon took a healthy swallow of morning pick-me-up. "I broke down on the side of the road the other day, and it was going to cost a bundle to get repairs, and they would only have been a patch job."

"How are you going to make the car payments when you have house payments and the cost of renovations?" Linc waved his hand to encompass the flashback-in-time kitchen. The yellow countertops and harvest gold built-in double oven. The brightly colored fruit-print textured wallpaper that Damon had started peeling off around the pantry door.

"I'm putting off the renovations for now and I'll work extra shifts if I have to." And he'd rack up the balance on his credit card in hopes of being able to pay it off sooner rather than later.

"Just put a pause on buying anything else big." The piece of folded cardboard used to level the table legs had been dislodged and the table wobbled, sloshing coffee over the rim of Linc's mug. "You should've bought furniture instead of a car."

"Linc, I'm not your kid brother anymore. I can handle my own life."

"Habit, I guess." They were quiet for a few minutes while they drank their coffee.

Damon rubbed his bare foot over the textured vinyl flooring that he couldn't wait to replace. But he could live with it for a while longer if he had to. "Speaking of renovations, how's the bookstore coming along?"

"Great. We're almost ready to open. Remi's big ideas for the children's book section will be worth the extra time and effort. Kids are going to love it. So, are you really going to babysit for Sari?"

"Yes. I lost our bet. I have to." He didn't mention that he wanted to hang out with her kids because he wanted to get to know their mom.

Linc's phone chimed with a text message, and he pulled it out to look at the screen. "I need to get going. I'm late."

"Maybe you shouldn't have stopped to nag your brother like an old woman."

"Nah. Sounds boring." Linc put his mug in the sink. "See you later."

Damon continued to sit at his rickety table with the uneven legs. He'd been looking forward to putting his own touch on this house, but he had to have a car to get around. True, it didn't necessarily have to be a car as expensive as the one he'd bought, but it was too late now. He'd lose too much money if he traded it in so soon.

He looked around the room at all the things he'd planned to change. Like raising the dropped ceiling that was covered with foam rectangles more suited to an office than a home. He was tall and more height in the room would help it not to feel so closed in. And the popcorn ceilings in the rest of the house needed a good scraping. Especially the room with the blue shag carpeting that had glitter mixed in with the popcorn. He could save money by doing a lot of the demo himself. But then who knew how long he'd have to wait to buy materials, and until then, he'd have to live in a dismantled house.

He got up for a coffee refill and took out some of his frustration by ripping off another strip of wallpaper. It tore with a very satisfying sound.

When he opened his refrigerator for something to eat, there was a very limited and unappealing selection. He had a couple of pieces of toast with the last of the strawberry jam, then got dressed for a trip to GreatStore. Grocery shopping was something he hated and normally put off as long as possible, but today it came with the possibility of seeing Sari.

As Damon pushed his shopping cart up and down the aisles, he kept an eye out for the beautiful woman who had starred in his dreams last night. She'd said she was working today, but she had not been at a front register, so he kept searching. He tossed chips and other snacks in his basket along with frozen meals, cans of soup, bread and peanut butter, and other sandwich makings.

When he came around a freestanding display of bakery items, he spotted Sari in the produce section and a lightness filled his chest. She was arranging vegetables, and today she was wearing dark jeans. They weren't skintight, but they were definitely not "mom" jeans. She wore them well.

As he was pushing his shopping cart over to where Sari worked, a woman he'd gone out with a couple of times waved from across the display of bananas.

Oh, man. Not now.

She headed his way. "I'm so happy to see you, Damon."

When she said his name in a voice too loud for the store, Sari turned her head and looked right at him just as he received a very enthusiastic hug. One he ordinarily would have welcomed, but not today. Not in front of a woman he was hoping to get to know better.

Sari jerked her head back to her work. Maybe she was jealous and didn't like seeing him with another woman. He could hope.

"You, too," he said to the woman hanging on to him. "How have you been?"

"Good. I'm starting at a new hospital in Dallas next week."

She continued talking about her nursing job, but he was only half listening. Something about this re-union happening in front of Sari made him edgy and uncomfortable. Sari didn't seem like the kind of woman who had time for a man who dated a lot of different women.

But that's who I am. That's what I do.

He shook off that thought for later consideration. "I'm glad you're excited about your new job."

He was anxious for this surprise meeting to end so he could talk to Sari before she disappeared to another part of the store. Thankfully, the interaction was brief and didn't involve any more hugging.

When he made it over to Sari, he was relieved when she turned and gave him a big smile.

"Hi, Damon."

"Good morning."

She leaned forward to study the items in his cart. "I hope you're in this section of the store because you plan to add at least a few healthy items to your cart."

"What?" he said in mock outrage. "You don't approve of my meal choices?"

"Well…there is room for improvement."

"I'm not the best cook in the world. So I'm kind of limited on what I buy." He pointed to an eggplant. "Take that for example. I would have no idea what to do with that."

"I guess that vegetable can be a bit of a challenge." She continued arranging the squash. "I make a pretty good eggplant Parmesan."

"Sounds like something I need to try." He grabbed a bag of the small easy-to-peel oranges and added them to his cart.

"Is that a subtle hint? Are you asking me to cook for you?"

He chuckled. "No, but I wouldn't turn down an invitation."

"You never know. It could happen." She dropped a couple of zucchini squash into a plastic bag and put them into his cart. "Chop these into bite-sized pieces, then sauté them with a little olive oil and whatever seasoning you like."

"Sounds easy enough." Her concern about his

health made him smile. No one had looked out for his eating since he'd lived under his mom's roof.

"Are you by any chance available to babysit this Saturday during the day?"

"I work Friday night, but I'm off on Saturday and would be happy to babysit. What do you have planned?"

"Alana asked me to do something with her, and I thought it might be a good chance for you to fulfill your promise. If you really are available."

"I am one hundred percent available," he said. "In every way."

Sari tried to hide her smile. "Cool. Is ten in the morning too early for you?"

"I can be there at ten. No problem." Before he could say more, a store manager was walking by and paused long enough to give Sari a look that Damon read as "get back to work."

"Text me your address because I better get out of here."

"I will."

As he pushed his cart toward the checkout, he overheard, "Sari, can I see you in my office?"

Damon winced, hoping he hadn't gotten her into trouble.

Chapter Four

"Benjy Keeling, do not even think about trapping your little brother under that laundry basket."

Her four-year-old froze with the plastic latticework basket hovering above his younger brother. Sari took it from him, and not for the first time, she considered canceling her day out with Alana. Leaving her boys with Damon was just asking for trouble of one kind or another.

"But Mama, he's a tiger," Benjy said with his hands held out like it should be totally obvious. "In zoos there's cages."

Her two-year-old, Jacob, shook his head of red curls and growled.

Sari chuckled and put the basket on the couch, loving that her boys were so good at playing pretend. "I can see that. Very fierce. Instead of a cage, what if you use your blocks to build a wall around Jacob the tiger?"

Benjy bounced on his toes. "A magic wall so he can't climb it?"

"What a good idea." She kissed the top of his head and ruffled Jacob's hair, making him growl again.

A knock at the door sent her pulse tripping.

He's early.

It was too late to call Damon and say she'd changed her mind. Sari peered through a crack in the vertical blinds. With his thumbs snagged in the back pockets of his jeans, Damon's shoulders were drawn back, enhancing the way his black T-shirt pulled taut across a broad chest and stretched around his biceps. A dark lock of his hair fell over his forehead, the morning sun making it shine. It was entirely possible he was going to be the one who caused trouble, not her toddlers. And she had a feeling she'd be the one who caught that trouble.

Her emotions had been close to the surface all morning, but now she was practically vibrating. Sari smoothed a hand over her hair and opened her front door. "Good morning."

"Hi, Sari." Damon took a step closer. "It's good to see you again."

"You, too." His laid-back grin managed to be both easygoing and a bit mysterious. Some might even use the word *sexy*. No wonder women chased him down in public to hug him. With no idea what he was thinking—and praying he couldn't read *her* thoughts—she told herself to calm down and go on with today's plans. Everyone said Damon was a good guy and they would trust him to look after their own children. She'd only be gone for a few hours.

"Have you changed your mind?" he asked.

"Oh, no. Sorry. Please come in." She stepped back and ushered him inside while heat washed over her face and neck. She'd been too busy overthinking and staring at him and of course managed to embarrass herself right out of the gate.

Her living room suddenly felt too small. Sensations she had attributed to a rare night out, a handsome man flirting with her and a couple of drinks were once again flooding through her system. Without any of that, her attraction to him was just as strong as it had been on Tuesday night. And after her imagination had run wild over the last few days, possibly stronger.

"Are you sure you're ready for this?" she asked him. "You haven't changed *your* mind?"

"Nope. I'm ready to give a busy mom a much-needed break."

That sweet statement touched her heart. Her boys walked into the room and came over to stand on either side of her, staring at this man much like she had done.

"This is Benjy, and this is Jacob." She put a hand on each of their heads in turn.

Damon knelt in front of them. "Hey, guys. I'm Damon. Can I hang out with y'all today?"

Jacob wrapped his arms around her leg and looked

up at her in that way that told her he was nervous about her leaving. She picked up her baby for a cuddle and kissed his forehead.

Benjy cocked his head. "You know how to play superhero?"

"Of course." Damon stood.

"Okay." Benjy grabbed Damon's hand, ready to pull him down the hallway to their bedroom.

"Wait," she said to her son. "I need to talk to Mr. Damon for a few minutes. Why don't we all sit down and get to know one another." She sat on one end of her gray couch and Damon sat on the other.

Jacob got comfortable on her lap and rested his head against her chest but kept a close eye on the new guy while Benjy started digging in a basket of toys in the corner.

"I hope I didn't get you into trouble at work yesterday. I couldn't help overhearing her asking you to come to her office."

"No, you didn't get me into any trouble. I had asked about how I might work up to a management position, and she was giving me some information. I can't keep going from one menial low-paying job to another. Eventually, I want to go back to college and finish the last two years of my accounting degree."

"Sounds like a very good plan."

"You mentioned growing up in a big family," Sari said. "I'm an only child and have always been fascinated with what it's like to have siblings. There are four of you?"

"Five. You know Linc. He is the oldest. Next is

Max, who I don't think you've met, and then Coop and me. We have one little sister, Justine. She was a single mom for most of her son's first year, and we were raised by a single mom. My dad was not around."

That's likely how he'd known she needed a break. She adjusted Jacob on her lap. "From what I can see so far, your mother did a good job."

"Thanks. Do you have family close by?"

"No. My parents were older when they had me. My mom was forty-five and my dad was fifty. I lost both of them within the last several years."

Benjy brought a book over and handed it to Damon. "Can you read?"

"I sure can."

With both hands on his hips, Benjy tipped his head. "Prove it."

Damon chuckled, but Sari gasped. "Benjy, you know that is not the way we talk to people. Especially not when you are asking for something."

"That's what the kids say at day care. They say, 'prove it' and 'don't be a chicken.'"

Sari hated that her kids had to go to day care, but she had no other option. The day care at Great-Store was the only one in her price range—unless she dipped into the money that she was saving for a rainy day. She knew better than a lot of people that you never could tell when a rainy day might turn into a flood. She had to stay prepared.

"Benjy, those are not things you say to an adult. Want to try again and ask Mr. Damon in a nice way?"

"Okay, Mama. Will you read to us, Mr. Damon?" Her sassy-pants four-year-old shot her a brief glance, then added one more thing to his request. "Please."

"I would be happy to read to you. Hop up here between me and your mom."

With more skill and flourish than she had expected, Damon read the short book about farm animals, making the boys giggle with his dramatic voices.

"The end," he said, and closed the book.

"Thank you." Benjy slid off the couch. "Gotta go potty."

Sari shifted her son on her lap. "Speaking of that. Jacob is doing really well with potty training, but he is still in Pull-Ups. You should ask him to try going potty about every thirty minutes."

"Good to know. And that's no problem. I've looked after my sister's son, Morgan."

"They live here in Chatelaine?"

"No. They live a few hours away in Rambling Rose, so I don't get to see them as much as I'd like."

With each minute they talked, and his willingness to share his life and family, she was feeling better about letting him babysit.

Jacob scooched off of her and crossed the center cushion to sit on Damon's lap. "Hi," he said in his cute baby voice.

"Hello, little buddy," Damon replied. "I like your green shirt."

Her youngest son did not take easily to many people, so this was a good sign, and she let herself relax a bit more.

Benjy came back into the room. "Now is it time to play?"

"Almost. Why don't you go get things ready in your room, and we will come find you before I leave."

Benjy took off down the hallway, but Jacob stayed on Damon's lap.

"You're worried about leaving, aren't you?" Damon said.

"Maybe a little."

"Please don't worry. We will get along fine. Like I said, I'm just a big kid myself."

She chuckled. "Is that supposed to make me feel better?"

"A very responsible kid." His teasing smile shifted into an understanding expression. "Sari, if you're truly not comfortable with this, we can cancel. The last thing I want to do is stress you out."

"A single mom is stressed out most of the time."

"I'm sure we can come up with some other way for me to pay my debt to you."

She could think of a few creative ways that would be fun for both of them. The direction her thoughts were taking with this man was an ill-advised path. "Since your references check out, I'm going to go ahead with my plans. I could use a break."

"Good call. You have to take care of yourself if you're going to be in any condition to take care of others."

"That is true. Let me show you where everything

is." When she stood, Jacob raised his arms to her, as if still wary about her leaving. She lifted him from Damon's lap and walked into the open-concept kitchen with her toddler on her hip. A handwritten schedule was held on to the refrigerator door with musical note magnets. "Here is their schedule and all the important numbers like Poison Control. Call me if anything happens or you have questions." She paused and looked him straight in the eye. "Why are you grinning at me like that?"

"No specific reason. You just make me smile." He used a pointer finger to tickle Jacob's tummy and made him giggle.

Needing some physical distance from his enticing leather and spices scent, she opened the refrigerator door as a barrier between them and tapped a finger on a stack of three plastic containers. "This is lunch for all three of you."

"You made lunch for me, too?"

"I did. I hope you like peanut butter and jelly." She pointed to another shelf. "And here are some sliced apples."

"Got it. No ordering pizza and beer." He was close enough that Jacob reached out to him, and Damon took him into his arms. "Are you ready to have some fun today, little buddy?"

Her baby nodded and stuck his thumb in his mouth.

He looked so small against Damon's broad chest. Since her kids didn't have a man or any father figure in their lives, this was an unusual sight. One she ached for her boys to have.

"What are your plans for the day?" Damon asked, breaking into her thoughts.

"A haircut and pedicure with Alana."

He gasped in a dramatic fashion that made Jacob giggle again. "You aren't cutting off your hair, are you?"

"No, just a trim. Don't forget that you can call me at any time." She grasped his arm. "I'm serious. Call me straightaway if you have any questions at all or if there is any problem. Even a small one."

He put his free hand on top of hers, and that's when she realized her fingers were wrapped around his wrist. She relaxed her grip and pulled away.

"Don't worry. I promise I'll call you if we need you."

"Mama," Benjy yelled from his bedroom. "Are you coming?"

She let out a slow breath and they all went down the hallway to the boys' room. "Benjy, what did I say about yelling in the house?"

"No yelling."

"That's right. The neighbors don't need to hear everything you say." She bent forward and opened her arms. "Give me a hug." Benjy hugged her, and she could feel his excitement to play with a new friend. She turned to give Jacob a hug, but with him in Damon's arms, she hesitated. Jacob leaned toward her, and she couldn't deny him a kiss. When she met Damon's brown eyes, he looked as if he was hoping for a kiss, too. And she was surprisingly tempted. Instead, Sari took a few steps backward, sending the message that there would be no kissing between the adults in the room.

"You two be good for Mr. Damon."

"We will, Mama," Benjy said, but the sideways glance and grin he gave Damon were a bit suspicious.

Jacob looked a little less sure about her leaving, but when Damon stuck out his tongue, then pulled each ear to make it go that direction before touching his nose to make his tongue disappear into his mouth, her two-year-old giggled.

"Have fun," Damon said to her, and the three of them waved as she went out the door of the bedroom.

"Mama said to be good, but does that mean I can't be the bad guy if we play pretend?"

"I think it's okay if it's pretend," Damon said.

Sari took a deep breath and locked the front door of her apartment behind her. The three of them had already taken to one another. They would be okay. She got into her ten-year-old blue Volvo and drove toward Alana's house.

I need to get my mind on something other than Damon.

Jacob wiggled to get down, and Damon set him on his feet beside his big brother. "What shall we do first?"

The four-year-old put his hands on his little brother's head. "We're playing zoo. Jacob is a tiger, and we have to build a magic wall so he can't get out and eat all the people."

Jacob dropped to all fours, growled and tried to bite his brother's leg.

"No biting." Benjy shook a finger at him.

"Do I get to be an animal, too?" Damon asked.

"Yes." Benjy turned in a circle as he talked. "What do you wanna be?"

"I want to be a polar bear."

"Okay. Do polar bears give rides on their backs? I like animal rides. Mama took us to ride a little horse at the fair. It went round and round." Benjy galloped around Damon in demonstration. "Next time I want it to go faster and faster."

Damon liked this kid's spirit. "Since I will be a well-trained bear, yes, I will give rides to kids at our zoo."

They used a variety of blocks and other toys to make the animal cages in the living room, and the boys magically changed back into people so they could have a ride on the polar bear's back. Damon's knees were beginning to hurt from crawling around with the added weight on his back, but their happy laughter and encouragement kept him going.

"Who is hungry?" he asked the boys.

"I am," Benjy said. "Can we have cake?"

"I don't think your mom left any cake, but we can pretend our peanut butter and jelly sandwiches are cake."

The little boy shook his head. "I don't pretend *that* good."

Damon chuckled and held Jacob's hand as they went into the kitchen for lunch. He once again looked at the handwritten schedule. Everything for Benjy was written in blue and Jacob's schedule was written with green ink. Very organized and thorough. Guess as a single parent, Sari had to be.

After handwashing, he got out the three containers with their sandwiches and the apple slices, poured drinks, and got everyone seated. He was very glad she had prepared lunch and he didn't have to cook. They talked about all the animals you could ride, and he only had to get up twice while they ate. Once for napkins, and then again to grab a towel when Benjy spilled his milk.

Damon helped Jacob down from his booster seat, took the plastic containers to the sink and started washing them out. While he was cleaning up from a lunch that got a little messier than he'd hoped, the boys played with the animal magnets on the lower half of the refrigerator, and he didn't notice when they moved to the pantry.

"It's snowing," Benjy announced in a loud voice.

"No," Jacob fussed.

Damon turned to see the boys standing in the open doorway of the pantry. With a big mischievous smile, Benjy was sprinkling a handful of flour on his little brother's head.

"Lots of snow," the four-year-old said.

Damon groaned. "Oh, no. Benjy, don't do that. Now we have another mess to clean up."

Jacob shook his head and ran to Damon with his

arms up. "You're okay, little buddy." He picked him up and held him over the sink while dusting flour from his hair.

"Superhero time," Benjy announced.

"Not until we clean up the mess you've made. Can you get the broom, please?"

The little boy sighed dramatically as if this was the worst idea ever, but he did as he was asked.

Because Damon had not thought to wash the boys' hands after eating, the broom handle was now sticky, and he had to clean that, too. Once the kitchen, pantry and children were clean, the three of them went to the boys' bedroom.

"Is it nap time?" he asked the boys in a hopeful tone.

"No. Superhero time." Benjy opened a drawer and started tossing costumes over his shoulder. "Which one you want?" he asked Damon.

"I don't think any of these will fit me. But we can come up with something." Damon pulled the top Batman sheet off one of the twin beds and tied it around his neck like a cape. "Is this good?"

Benjy shook his head and sat beside the pile of costumes. "You need more. Jacob, you be Cat Boy."

Damon helped Jacob into a black cat Halloween costume and buckled a plastic utility belt around his waist. "There you go, little buddy. Super Cat Boy."

The two-year-old got on all fours and started crawling around while meowing.

Benjy had his legs in the air as he pulled on a Spider-Man costume. "Mama said we can't have a real cat. No pets in the 'partment."

"That's too bad. I like cats, too," Damon said. "We had one when I was a kid. It was orange and had a crooked tail."

"I want a black cat," Benjy said.

Jacob shook his head. "No, no, no. Purpur cat."

"He means purple, but that's not a real thing," Benjy clarified.

Damon tapped a finger against his chin. "Are you sure? Maybe purple cats are just very rare."

"I don't think so. I've never seen a purple cat."

"Purpur cat," Jacob repeated.

"I'm shooting webs and flying," Benjy yelled, and started jumping on the bed.

As he attempted a leap from one twin bed to the other, Damon caught him midair and put him on the floor. "I bet you are not supposed to be jumping on the bed. Am I right?" He really did not want them getting hurt on his watch. Then he'd be the one in trouble and Sari would never want to go out with him.

The little boy fell back onto the bed. "No yelling. No jumping on the bed. No fun."

Damon covered his mouth to hide his amusement. "I think we can still have tons of fun. Can I be Superman?"

The four-year-old sat up and shook his head. "You're Superboy."

"Okay. Now, I need to add to my superhero costume, and I have an idea. I need to go to the pantry and get the tinfoil."

While they played, Damon couldn't help wondering where their father was. Was he part of their lives or was he completely out of the picture? He didn't feel comfortable asking the kids.

At nap time, the boys insisted he continue to wear his superhero costume while he sat on the floor between their twin beds and read to them. Four books later, they were both asleep. He eased to his feet, then stepped out of their room, closing the door as quietly as possible. Hopefully he had time to clean up a bit before Sari got home. He wanted to show her he hadn't been kidding about being able to do this.

Soft female laughter made him turn with a jerk. Sari was standing at the end of the short hallway, and she was grinning from ear to ear.

Don't miss
Fortune's Fatherhood Dare *by Makenna Lee,*
available April 2023 wherever
Harlequin® Special Edition
books and ebooks are sold.

www.Harlequin.com

COMING NEXT MONTH FROM

(H) HARLEQUIN®
SPECIAL EDITION™

#2977 SELF-MADE FORTUNE
The Fortunes of Texas: Hitting the Jackpot • by Judy Duarte
Heiress Gigi Fortune has the hots for her handsome new lawyer! Harrison Vasquez may come from humble beginnings, but they have so much fun—in and out of bed! If only she can convince him their opposite backgrounds are the perfect ingredients for a shared future...

#2978 THE MARINE'S SECOND CHANCE
The Camdens of Montana • by Victoria Pade
The worst wound Major Dalton Camden ever received was the day Marli Abbott broke his heart. Now the fate of Marli's brother is in his hands...and Marli's back in town, stirring up all their old emotions. This time, they'll have to revisit the good *and* the bad to make their second-chance reunion permanent.

#2979 LIGHTNING STRIKES TWICE
Hatchet Lake • by Elizabeth Hrib
Newly single Kate Cardiff is in town to care for her sick father and his ailing ranch. The only problem? Annoying—and annoyingly sexy—ranch hand Nathan Prescott. Nathan will use every tool at his disposal to win over love-shy Kate. Starting with his knee-weakening kisses...

#2980 THE TROUBLE WITH EXES
The Navarros • by Sera Taíno
Dr. Nati Navarro's lucrative grant request is under review—by none other than her ex Leo Espinoza. But Leo is less interested in holding a grudge and much more interested in exploring their still-sizzling connection. Can Nati's lifelong dream include a career *and* romance this time around?

#2981 A CHARMING SINGLE DAD
Charming, Texas • by Heatherly Bell
How dare Rafe Reyes marry someone else! Jordan Del Toro knows she should let bygones be bygones. But when a wedding brings her face-to-face with her now-divorced ex—and his precious little girl—Jordan must decide if she wants revenge... or a new beginning with her old flame.

#2982 STARTING OVER AT TREVINO RANCH
Peach Leaf, Texas • by Amy Woods
Gina Heron wants to find a safe refuge in her small Texas hometown—*not* in Alex Trevino's strong arms. But reuniting with the boy she left behind is more powerful and exhilarating than a mustang stampede. The fiery-hot chemistry is still there. But can she prove she's no longer the cut-and-run type?

YOU CAN FIND MORE INFORMATION ON UPCOMING HARLEQUIN TITLES, FREE EXCERPTS AND MORE AT HARLEQUIN.COM.

HSECNM0323

HARLEQUIN
PLUS

Try the best multimedia
subscription service for romance
readers like you!

Read, Watch and Play.

Experience the easiest way to get
the romance content you crave.

Start your **FREE TRIAL** at
<u>www.harlequinplus.com/freetrial</u>.